I own you . . .

"You're crazy," Cassie told Faye bluntly. "And," she added, "our deal is finished. I did what you asked: I brought you the skull. You used it and you almost got killed. So now it's over."

Faye's lazy expression disappeared. "Oh, no, Cassie," she said. The hint of a smile curved her lips, but her eyes were predatory. Ruthless. "It's only starting. Don't you see?" She began to laugh. "You're more my captive now than ever. It's not just Adam anymore—now I can tell Diana about *this*. How do you think the Princess of Purity is going to feel when she finds out her 'little sister' stole the skull?"

BOOKS BY L. J. SMITH

THE VAMPIRE DIARIES

Volume I: The Awakening

Volume II: The Struggle

Volume III: The Fury

Volume IV: Dark Reunion

THE SECRET CIRCLE TRILOGY

Volume I: The Initiation

Volume II: The Captive

Volume III: The Power

The Night of the Solstice

Heart of Valor

Published by HarperPrism

The Secret Circle

Volume II

The Captive

L. J. Smith

HarperPrism
A Division of HarperCollinsPublishers

HarperPrism
A Division of HarperCollinsPublishers
10 East 53rd Street, New York, NY 10022–5299

A mass market edition of this book was published in 1992 by
HarperPaperbacks.

Produced by Daniel Weiss Associates, Inc.,
33 West 17th Street, New York, NY 10011.

First HarperPrism printing: September 1999

Printed in the United States of America

ISBN 0-06-106715-6

❖ 10 9 8 7

For my father,
the parfit gentil knight

The Captive

ONE

Fire, Cassie thought. All around her she saw blazing autumn colors. The yellow-orange of sugar maple, the brilliant red of sassafras, the crimson of sumac bushes. It was as if the entire world was flaming with Faye's element.

And I'm trapped in the middle of it.

The sick feeling in the pit of Cassie's stomach got worse with every step she took down Crowhaven Road.

The yellow Victorian house at the bottom of the road looked as pretty as ever. Sunlight was striking rainbow sparks off a prism that hung in the highest tower window. A girl with long, light-brown hair called out from the porch.

"Hurry up, Cassie! You're late!"

"Sorry," Cassie called back, trying to hurry when what she really wanted to do was turn around and run the other way. She had the sudden, inexplicable conviction that her private thoughts must show in her face. Laurel would take one look at her and know all about what had happened with Adam last night, and all about the bargain with Faye.

But Laurel just grabbed her by the waist and hustled her inside and upstairs to Diana's bedroom. Diana was standing in front of the large walnut cabinet; Melanie was sitting on the bed. Sean was perched uneasily in the window seat, rubbing his knees with his palms.

Adam was standing beside him.

He looked up as Cassie came in.

Cassie met those blue-gray eyes for only an instant, but it was long enough. They were the color of the ocean at its most mysterious, sunlit on the surface but with incomprehensible depths underneath. The rest of his face was the same as ever: arresting and intriguing, pride showing in the high cheekbones and determined mouth, but sensitivity and humor showing there too. His face looked different only because last night Cassie had seen those eyes midnight blue with passion, and had felt

2

that mouth . . .

Not by word or look or deed, she told herself fiercely, staring down at the ground because she didn't dare look up again. But her heart was pounding so hard she expected to see the front of her sweater fluttering. Oh, God, how was she ever going to be able to carry this off and keep her vow? It took an incredible amount of energy to sit down by Melanie and not look at him, to block the charismatic heat of his presence out of her mind.

You'd better get used to it, she told herself. Because you're going to be doing a lot of it from now on.

"Good; we're all here," Diana said. She went over and shut the door. "This is a closed meeting," she went on, turning back to the group. "The others weren't invited because I'm not sure they have the same interests at heart as we do."

"That's putting it mildly," Laurel said under her breath.

"They're going to be upset if they find out," Sean said, his black eyes darting between Adam and Diana.

"Then let them be," Melanie said unemotionally. Her own cool gray eyes fixed on

3

Sean and he flushed. "This is much more important than any fit Faye can throw. We have to find out what happened to that dark energy . . . and now."

"I think I know a way," said Diana. Out of a white velvet pouch she took a delicate green stone on a silver chain.

"A pendulum," Melanie said at once.

"Yes. This is peridot," Diana said to Cassie. "It's a visionary stone—right, Melanie? Usually we use clear quartz as a pendulum, but this time I think the peridot is better—more likely to pick up traces of the dark energy. We'll take it down to the place where the dark energy escaped and it'll align itself in the direction the energy went and start swinging."

"We hope," Laurel murmured.

"Well, that's the theory," Melanie said.

Diana looked at Adam, who had been unusually quiet. "What do you think?"

"I think it's worth a try. It'll take a lot of mental power to back it up, though. We'll all have to concentrate—especially since we're not a full Circle." His voice was calm and even, and Cassie admired him for it. She kept her face turned in Diana's direction, though as a matter of fact her eyes were fixed on the walnut cabinet.

Diana turned to Cassie. "What about you?"

"Me?" Cassie said, startled, tearing her eyes away from the cabinet door. She hadn't expected to be asked; she didn't know anything about pendulums or peridot. To her horror, she felt her face redden.

"Yes, you. You might be new to the methods we use, but a lot of the time you have *feelings* about things."

"Oh. Well . . ." Cassie tried to search her feelings, scrabbling to get beyond the guilt and terror that were uppermost. "I think . . . it's a good idea," she said finally, knowing how lame that sounded. "It seems fine to me."

Melanie rolled her eyes, but Diana nodded as seriously as she had at Adam. "All right, then, the only thing to do is try," she said, dropping the peridot and its silver chain into the palm of her left hand and clasping it tightly. "Let's go."

Cassie couldn't breathe; she was still reeling from the impact of Diana's clear green eyes, slightly darker than the peridot, but with that same delicate transparency, as if there were light shining behind them.

I can't do it, she thought. She was surprised at how stark and simple everything was now that she had actually looked Diana in the eyes.

I *can't* do it. I'll have to tell Faye—no, I'll tell Diana. That's it. I'll tell Diana myself before Faye can, and I'll *make* her believe me. She'll understand; Diana is so good, she'll have to understand.

Everyone had gotten up. Cassie got up too, turning toward the door to hide her agitation—*should I tell her right now? Ask her to stay back a minute?*—when the door flew open in her face.

Faye was standing in the doorway.

Suzan and Deborah were behind her. The strawberry-blonde looked mean, and the biker's habitual scowl was even darker than usual. Behind *them* were the Henderson brothers, Chris frowning and Doug grinning in a wild way that was disturbing.

"Going somewhere without us?" Faye said. She was speaking to Diana, but her eyes remained fixed on Cassie.

"Not now," Laurel muttered.

Diana let out a deep breath. "I didn't think you'd be interested," she said. "We're going to trace the dark energy."

"Not *interested*? When all the rest of you are so busy? Of course, I can only speak for myself, but I'm interested in everything the Circle does. What about you, Deborah?"

The biker girl's scowl changed briefly into a malicious grin. "I'm interested," she said.

"And what about you, Suzan?"

"*I'm* interested," Suzan chimed in.

"And what about you, Chris?"

"*I'm*—"

"All *right*," Diana said. Her cheeks were flushed; Adam had come to stand at her side. "We get the point. We're better off with a full Circle, anyway—but where's Nick?"

"I have no idea," Faye said coolly. "He's not at home."

Diana hesitated, then shrugged. "We'll do our best with what we have," she said. "Let's go down to the garage."

She gestured at Melanie and Laurel and they went first, elbowing past Faye's group, who looked as if they wanted to stay and argue some more. Adam took charge of Sean and got him out the door, then began herding the Hendersons. Deborah and Suzan looked at Faye, then followed the guys.

Cassie had been hanging back, hoping for the chance to speak to Diana alone. But Diana seemed to have forgotten her; she was engaged in a staredown with Faye. Finally, head high, she walked past the tall girl who was still semiblocking the doorway.

"Diana . . ." Faye called. Diana didn't look back, but her shoulders tensed: she was listening.

"You're going to lose them all," Faye said, and she chuckled her lazy chuckle as Diana went on to the staircase.

Biting her lip, Cassie stepped forward furiously. One good shove in Faye's middle, she was thinking. But Faye rounded smoothly on her, blocking the doorway completely.

"Oh, no, you don't. We need to talk," she said.

"I don't want to talk to you."

Faye ignored her. "Is it in here?" She moved quickly to the walnut cabinet and pulled at a handle, but the drawer was locked. They all were. "Damn. But you can find out where she keeps the key. I want it as soon as possible, do you understand?"

"Faye, you're not listening to me! I've changed my mind. I'm not going to do it after all."

Faye, who had been prowling around the room like a panther, taking advantage of this unique opportunity to examine Diana's things, stopped in her tracks. Then she turned slowly to Cassie, and smiled.

"Oh, Cassie," she said. "You really kill me."

"I'm *serious*. I've changed my mind." Faye just smiled at her, leaning back against the wall and shaking her head. Her heavy-lidded golden eyes were glowing with amusement, her mane of pitch-black hair fell across her shoulders as her head moved. She had never looked more beautiful—or more dangerous.

"Cassie, come here." Faye's voice was just slightly edged with impatience, like a teacher who's put up with a lot from a backward student. "Let me show you something," Faye went on, catching Cassie's elbow and dragging her to the window. "Now, look down there. What do you see?"

Cassie stopped fighting and looked. She saw the Club, the in-crowd at New Salem high school, the kids who awed—and terrorized— students and teachers alike. She saw them gathered in Diana's driveway, their heads gleaming in the first rays of sunset: Suzan's strawberry blond turned to red, Deborah's dark curls touched with ruby, Laurel's long, light-brown hair and Melanie's short auburn and the Henderson brothers' disheveled yellow all highlighted by the ruddy glow in the sky.

And she saw Adam and Diana, standing close, Diana's silvery head drooping to Adam's shoulder. He was holding her protectively, his own hair dark as wine.

Faye's voice came from behind Cassie. "If you tell her, you'll kill her. You'll destroy her faith in everything she's ever believed in. And you'll take away the only thing she has to trust, to rely on. Is that what you want?"

"Faye . . ." Cassie seethed.

"And, incidentally, you'll get yourself banished from the Club. You know that, don't you? How do you think Melanie and Laurel are going to feel when they hear that you messed around with Diana's boyfriend? None of them will ever speak to you again, not even to make a full Circle. The coven will be destroyed too."

Cassie's teeth were clenched. She wanted to hit Faye, but it wouldn't do any good. Because Faye was right. And Cassie thought she could stand being blackballed, being a pariah at school again; she even thought she could stand to destroy the coven. But the picture of Diana's face . . .

It *would* kill Diana. By the time Faye got finished telling it her way, it would. Cassie's fantasy of confessing to Diana and having

Diana understand vanished like a pricked soap bubble.

"And what I want is so reasonable," Faye was going on, almost crooning. "I just want to look at the skull for a little while. I know what I'm doing. You'll get it for me, won't you, Cassie? Won't you? Today?"

Cassie shut her eyes. Against her closed eyelids the light was red as fire.

O

TWO

Somewhere on the way downstairs Cassie stopped feeling guilty.

She didn't know exactly how it happened. But it was *necessary*, if she was going to survive this. She was doing everything she could to protect Diana—and Adam, too, in a way. Adam must never know about Faye's blackmail. So Cassie would do whatever it took to protect them both, but by God, she wasn't going to feel guilty on top of it.

And she had to handle Faye somehow as well, she thought, marching behind the tall girl, past Diana's father's study. She had to keep Faye from doing anything too radical with the skull. She didn't know how; she'd have to think about that later. But somehow she would do it.

If Faye had looked back just then, Cassie thought, she might have been surprised to see the face of the girl behind her. For the first time in her life Cassie felt as if her eyes were hard, like the blue steel of a revolver instead of the soft blue of wildflowers.

But right now she had to look neutral—composed. The group on the driveway looked up as she and Faye came out the door.

"What took you so long?" Laurel asked.

"We were plotting to kill you all," Faye said breezily. "Shall we?" She gestured toward the garage.

There were only traces of yesterday's chalk circle left on the floor. Once again the garage was empty of cars—they were lucky Diana's father worked so much at his law firm.

Diana, her left fist still closed, went over to the wall of the garage, directly behind the place Cassie had been sitting when they had performed the skull ceremony. Cassie followed her and then drew in her breath sharply.

"It's *burned*." She hadn't noticed that last night. Well, of course not; it had been too dark.

Diana was nodding. "I hope nobody is going to keep arguing about whether there was any dark energy or not," she said, with a glance back at Deborah and Suzan.

The wood and plaster of the garage wall was charred in a circle perhaps a foot and a half in diameter. Cassie looked at it, and then at the remnants of the chalk circle on the floor. She had been sitting there, but part of her had been inside the skull. Diana had told them all to look into it, to concentrate, and suddenly Cassie had found herself inside it. That was where she'd seen—felt—the dark power. It had begun rushing outward, getting bigger, determined to break out of the crystal. And she'd seen a face. . . .

She was grateful, suddenly, for Adam's calm voice. "Well, we know what direction it started in, anyway. Let's see if the crystal agrees."

They were all standing around Diana. She looked at them, then held her left fist out, palm up, and unclasped her fingers. She took the top of the silver chain with her right hand and drew it up taut, so that the peridot just rested on her palm.

"Concentrate," she said. "Earth and Air,

help us see what we need to see. Show the traces of the dark energy to us. Everybody concentrate on the crystal."

Earth and Air, wind and tree, show us what we need to see, Cassie thought, her mind automatically setting the simple concept in a rhyme. The wood of the wall, the air outside; those were what they needed to help them. She found herself murmuring the words under her breath and quickly stopped, but Diana's green eyes flashed at her.

"Go on," Diana said tensely in a low voice, and Cassie started up again, feeling self-conscious.

Diana removed the hand that was supporting the crystal.

It spun on the chain, twirling until the chain was kinked tightly, and then twirling the other way. Cassie watched the pale green blur, murmuring the couplet faster and faster. *Earth and Air* . . . no, it was useless. The peridot was just spinning madly like a top gone wild.

Suddenly, with broad, sweeping strokes, the crystal began swinging back and forth.

Someone's breath hissed on the other side of the circle.

The peridot had straightened out; it was no

longer twirling, but swinging steadily and hard. Like a pendulum, Cassie realized. Diana wasn't doing it; the hand that held the chain remained steady. But the peridot was swinging hard, back toward the center of the chalk circle on the floor, and forward toward the burned place on the wall.

"Bingo," Adam said softly.

"We've got it," Melanie whispered. "All right, now you're going to have to move it out of alignment to get outside. Walk—carefully— to the door, and then try to come back to this exact place on the other side of the wall."

Diana wet her lips and nodded, then, holding the silver chain always at the same distance from her body, she turned smoothly and did as Melanie said. The coven broke up to give her room and regrouped around her outside. Finding the right place wasn't hard; there was another burned circle on the outer wall, somewhat fainter than the one inside.

As Diana brought the crystal into alignment once more, it began to swing again. Straight toward the burned place, straight out. Down Crowhaven Road, toward the town.

A shudder went up Cassie's spine.

Everyone looked at everyone else.

Holding the crystal away from her, Diana followed the direction of the swinging. They all fell in behind her, although Cassie noticed that Faye's group kept to the rear. Cassie herself was still fighting every second to *not* watch Adam.

Trees rustled overhead. Red maple, beech, slippery elm—Cassie could identify many of them now. But she tried to keep her eyes on the rapid swish of the pendulum.

They walked and walked, following the curve of Crowhaven Road down toward the water. Now grasses and hedges grew poorly in the sandy soil. The pale green stone was swinging at an angle, and Diana turned to follow it.

They were heading west now, along a deeply rutted dirt road. Cassie had never been this way before, but the other members of the Circle obviously had—they were exchanging guarded glances. Cassie saw a chain-link fence ahead, and then an irregular line of headstones.

"Oh, great," Laurel muttered from beside Cassie, and from somewhere in back Suzan said, "I don't believe this. First we have to walk for miles, and now . . ."

"What's the problem? Just gonna visit some of our ancestors underground," Doug

Henderson said, his blue-green eyes glittering oddly.

"Shut up," Adam said.

Cassie didn't want to go inside. She'd seen many cemeteries in New England—it seemed there was one on every other street in Massachusetts, and she'd been to Kori's funeral down in the town. This one didn't look any different from the others: it was a small, square plot of land cluttered with modest gravestones, many of them worn almost completely smooth with time. But Cassie could hardly make herself follow the others onto the sparse, browning grass between the graves.

Diana led them straight down the middle of the cemetery. Most of the stones were small, scarcely reaching higher than Cassie's knees. They were shaped like arches, with two smaller arches on either side.

"Whoever carved these had a gruesome sense of humor," she breathed. Many of the stones were etched with crude skulls, some of them winged, others in front of crossbones. One had an entire skeleton, holding a sun and moon in its hands.

"Death's victory," Faye said softly, so close that Cassie felt warmth on the nape of her

18

neck. Cassie jumped, but refused to look back.

"Oh, *terrific*," said Laurel as Diana slowed.

The light was dying from the sky. They were in the center of the graveyard, and a cool breeze blew over the stunted grass, bringing a faint tang of salt with it. The hairs on the back of Cassie's neck were tingling.

You're a witch, she reminded herself. You should love cemeteries. They're probably your natural habitat.

The thought didn't really make her feel less frightened, but now her fear was mingled with something else—a sort of strange excitement. The darkness gathering in the sky and in the corners of the graveyard seemed closer. She was part of it, part of a whole new world of shadows and power.

Diana stopped.

The silver chain was a thin line in the gloom, with a pale blob below it. But Cassie could see that the peridot was no longer swinging like a pendulum. Instead it was moving erratically, round and round in circles. It would swing a few times one way, then slow and swing back the other way.

Cassie looked at it, then up at Diana's face. Diana was frowning. Everyone was watching the circling stone in dead silence.

Cassie couldn't stand the suspense any longer. "What does it *mean?*" she hissed to Laurel, who just shook her head. Diana, though, looked up.

"Something's wrong with it. It led here—and then it just stopped. But if we've found the place, it shouldn't be moving at all. The stone should just sort of point and quiver—right, Melanie?"

"Like a good hound dog," Doug said, with his wild grin.

Melanie ignored him. "That's the theory," she said. "But we've never really tried this before. Maybe it means . . ." Her voice trailed off as she looked around the graveyard, then she shrugged. "I don't know what it means."

The tingling at the back of Cassie's neck was getting stronger. The dark energy had come here—and done what? Disappeared? Dissipated? Or . . .

Laurel was breathing quickly, her elfin face unusually tense. Cassie instinctively moved a little closer to her. She and Laurel and Sean were the juniors, the youngest members of the Circle, and witch or not, Cassie's arms had broken out in gooseflesh.

"What if it's still here, somewhere . . . *waiting?*" she said.

"I doubt it," Melanie said, her voice as level and uninflected as usual. "It couldn't hang around without being stored somehow; it would just evaporate. It either came here and *did* something, or—" Again, though, she could only finish her sentence with a shrug.

"But what could it do here? I don't see any signs of damage, and I feel . . ." Still frowning, Diana caught the circling peridot in her left hand and held it. "This place feels confused—strange—but I don't sense any harm the dark energy has done. Cassie?"

Cassie tried to search her own feelings. Confusion—as Diana said. And she felt dread and anger and all sorts of churned-up emotions—but maybe that was just *her.* She was in no state to get a clear reading on anything.

"I don't know," she had to say to Diana. "I don't like it here."

"Maybe, but that's not the point. The point is that we don't see any burns the dark energy could have left, or sense anything it's destroyed or hurt," Diana said.

Deborah's voice was impatient. "Why are

you asking *her*, anyway?" she said with a jerk of her dark head toward Cassie. "She's hardly even one of us—"

"Cassie's as much a part of the Circle as you are," Adam interrupted, unusually curt. Cassie saw the arch, amused glance Faye threw him and wanted to intervene, but Diana was agreeing heatedly with Adam, and Deborah was bridling, glaring at both of them. It looked as if an argument would break out.

"Be quiet!" Laurel said sharply. "Listen!"

Cassie heard it as soon as the voices died down; the quiet crunch of gravel at the roadside. It was noticeable only against the deathly quiet of the autumn twilight.

"Somebody's coming," Chris Henderson said. He and Doug were poised for a fight.

They were all hideously on edge, Cassie realized. The crunch of footsteps sounded as loud as firecrackers now, grating against her taut nerves. She saw a dim shape beside the road, and then saw Adam move forward, so that he was in front of both Diana and her. I'm going to have to talk to him about that, she thought irrelevantly.

There was a pause in the footsteps, and the dim shape came toward them. Adam and the

Henderson brothers looked ready to rush it. Quarrel forgotten, Deborah looked ready too. Sean was cowering behind Faye. Cassie's heart began to pound.

Then she noticed a spot of red like a tiny burning coal floating near the figure, and she heard a familiar voice.

"If you want me, you got me. Four against one ought to be about fair."

With a whoop, Chris Henderson rushed forward. "Nick!"

Doug grinned, while still managing to look as if he might jump the approaching figure. Adam relaxed and stepped back.

"You sure, Adam? We can settle this right here," Nick said as he reached the group, the end of his cigarette glowing as he inhaled. Adam's eyes narrowed, and then Cassie saw the daredevil smile he'd worn at Cape Cod, when four guys with a gun had been chasing him. What was wrong with him, what was wrong with everybody tonight? she wondered. They were all acting crazy.

Diana put a restraining hand on Adam's arm. "No fighting," she said quietly.

Nick looked at her, then shrugged. "Kind of nervous, aren't you?" he said, surveying the group.

Sean emerged from behind Faye. "I'm just high-strung."

"Yes, you ought to be—from a tree," Faye said contemptuously.

Nick didn't smile, but then Nick never smiled. As always, his face was handsome but cold. "Well, maybe you have a reason to be nervous—at least some of you," he said.

"What's that supposed to mean? We came here looking for the dark energy that escaped last night," said Adam.

Nick went still, as if struck by a new idea, then his cigarette glowed again. "Maybe you're looking in the wrong place," he said expressionlessly.

Diana's voice was quiet. "Nick, will you please just tell us what you mean?"

Nick looked around at them all. "I mean," he said deliberately, "that while you've been scurrying around here, a crew's been up at Devil's Cove, pulling rocks off old Fogle."

Fogle? Cassie couldn't place the name. And then suddenly she saw it in her mind's eye—on a brass plate in a wood-paneled office. "Our principal?" she gasped.

"You got it. They say he got caught in an *avalanche*."

"An avalanche?" demanded Laurel in disbelief. "Around here?"

"How else do you explain the two-ton chunk of granite that was on top of him? Not to mention all the smaller stuff."

There was a moment of shocked silence.

"Is he . . ." Cassie couldn't finish the question.

"He wasn't looking too good when they got that chunk off him," Nick said, and then, with less sarcasm, "He's been dead since last night."

"Oh, God," Laurel whispered. There was another silence, just as shocked and even longer this time. Cassie knew they were all seeing the same thing: A crystal skull surrounded by a protective ring of candles—and one of the candles going out.

"It was Faye's fault," Sean began in a whine, but Faye interrupted without looking at him. "It was *his* fault."

"Wait, wait," said Diana. "We don't know the dark energy had anything to do with it. How *could* it have, when we know it came here and then stopped?"

"I don't think that's much comfort," Melanie said in a low voice. "Because if it wasn't the dark energy, who was it?"

25

There was a sort of strange shifting in the group, as if everyone was standing back and looking at all the others. Cassie felt a void in the pit of her stomach again. The principal was—had been—an outsider, who hated witches. And that meant they all had a motive—especially anybody who blamed the outsiders for Kori Henderson's death. Cassie looked at Deborah, and then at Chris and Doug.

Most of the rest of the coven was doing the same. Doug glared back, then gave a wild, defiant grin.

"Maybe we did do it," he said, eyes glittering.

"Did we?" said Chris, looking confused.

Deborah just looked scornful.

There was another silence, then Suzan spoke in a petulant voice. "Look, it's too bad about Fogle, but do we have to stand here forever? My feet are killing me."

Adam seemed to shake himself. "She's right; we should get out of this place. There's nothing we can do here." He put an arm around Diana, and gestured everybody else ahead. Cassie lingered. There was something she wanted to say to Diana.

But Diana was moving now, and Cassie

didn't have a chance. With the Henderson brothers in the lead, the group was taking a different route than the one they had taken in, cutting toward the northeast corner of the cemetery. As they approached the road, Cassie noticed the ground sloped up. There was a strange mound of grassy earth near the chain-link fence on this side; she almost tripped when she reached it. But even stranger was what she saw when they had passed it and she looked back.

The front of the mound was faced with stone slabs, and there was an iron door, maybe two feet square, set between them. The door had an iron hinge and a padlock on it, but it couldn't have opened anyway. Pushed right up against it was a large, irregular hunk of cement. Grass was growing up around the cement, showing it had been there a while.

Cassie's hands were icy cold, her heart was thudding, and she was dizzy. She tried to think, noticing with only part of her mind that she was passing by newer gravestones now, marble slabs with writing not worn smooth by time. She was trying to figure out what was wrong with her—was it just reaction to all the events of the past day and night? Was that why she was shaking?

"Cassie, are you okay?" Diana and Adam had turned around. Cassie was grateful for the growing darkness as she faced both of them and tried to get her mind clear.

"Yeah. I just—felt weird for a minute. But wait, Diana." Cassie remembered what she had wanted to say. "You know how you were asking me about my feelings before . . . well, I have a feeling about Mr. Fogle. I think the dark energy did have something to do with it, somehow. But . . ." She stopped. "But I don't know. There's something else strange going on."

"You can say that again," Adam said, and he reached for her arm to get her moving once more. Cassie evaded him and shot him a reproachful glance while Diana was staring into the distance. He looked at his own hand, startled.

There *was* something strange going on, something stranger than any of them realized, Cassie thought. "What is that thing back there, with the iron door?" she asked.

"It's been there for as long as I can remember," Diana said absently. "Something to do with storage, I think."

Cassie glanced back, but by now the mound was lost in darkness. She hugged herself, tucking her hands under her clasping arms to warm them. Her heart was still thudding.

I'll ask Grandma Howard about it, she decided. Whatever it was, it wasn't a storage shed, she knew that.

Then she noticed that Diana was toying with something around her neck as she walked lost in thought. It was a fine golden chain, and at the end of it dangled a key.

THREE

"I think," Melanie said quietly, "that it's time to talk about the skull. Adam's never told us exactly how he found it—"

"No, you've been very secretive about that," Faye put in.

"—but maybe now is the time."

Diana and Adam looked at each other, and then Diana nodded slightly. "All right, then, tell it. Try not to leave anything out."

After the walk back from the cemetery they had crowded, all twelve of them, into Diana's room. Cassie looked around at the group and realized that it was divided. Suzan, Deborah, and the Henderson brothers were sitting on one side, near Faye, while Laurel, Melanie, Adam, and Sean were on the other side, near Diana.

At least, Cassie thought, watching Sean's uneasily shifting eyes, Sean was sitting on Diana's side for the moment. He could change any time. And so could Nick—Nick could vote with Diana one day, and then for no apparent reason vote with Faye the next. Nick was always an unknown factor.

And so, a voice inside her whispered, are you.

But *that* was ridiculous. Nothing—not even Faye—could make Cassie vote against Diana. Not when it really counted.

Adam was talking in a low, thoughtful voice, as if he were trying to remember precisely. "It wasn't off Cape Cod, it was farther north, closer to Boston. Everybody knows there are seventeen islands off Boston Bay; they're all deserted and covered with weeds. Well, I found an eighteenth. It wasn't like the others; it was flat and sandy and there was no sign that people had ever been there. And there was something strange about it. . . . I'd been to the place before, but I'd never seen it. It was as if my eyes had suddenly been opened after—" He stopped.

Cassie, looking at the lamp's reflection on

Diana's gleaming pine-board floor, felt as if she were smothering. She didn't dare breathe until Adam went on, "—after working on the fishing boats all summer. But when I tried to head for the island, the tiller bucked, trying to keep me away or run me aground on the rocks. I had to wrestle with it to bring the boat in—and I had to call on Earth and Water or I'd never have made it. When I was finally safe I looked at the rocks and saw the wreckage of other boats. Anybody that had made it there before didn't make it away again alive." He took a deep, slow breath.

"As soon as I stepped on the sand I could *feel* that the whole island was electric. I knew it was the place even before I saw the circle of stones in the middle. It was just the way Black John described it. Sea heather had grown up around the rocks, but the center was clear and that's where I dug. About a minute later my shovel hit something hard."

"And then?" said Diana.

"And then I pulled it out. I felt—I don't know, dizzy, when I saw it. The sun was glittering on the sand and it sort of blinded me. Then I wrapped the skull up in my shirt and left. The island didn't fight when I went; it was like a trap that had been sprung. That was—let's see, September twenty-first. As soon as I got back to the Bay, I wanted to start up to New Salem, but I had some things to take care of. I couldn't get started until the next day, and I knew I was going to be late for Kori's initiation." He paused and threw an apologetic glance toward Doug and Chris.

They said nothing, but Cassie felt eyes flicker toward her. Kori's initiation had become Cassie's initiation, because on that morning Kori had been found dead at the bottom of the high-school steps.

"Just what is the point of all this storytelling?" Faye asked, her husky voice bored. "Unless"—she straightened up, looking more interested—"you think the rest of the Master Tools may be on that island."

"I told you before," Adam said. "There was nothing else there, Faye. Just the skull."

"And the point is that we need to know more about the skull," Diana put in. "For better or worse, we're stuck with it now. I don't think we should put it back on the island—"

"Put it *back*!" Faye exclaimed.

"—where anybody might find it, now that the protective spell is broken. It's not safe there. I don't know if it will be safe anywhere."

"Well, now," Faye murmured, looking sleepy. "If it's too much trouble for you, *I'll* be glad to take care of it."

Diana just shot her a look that said Faye was the last person she'd ask to take care of the skull. But, Cassie noticed with a sinking feeling, Faye's heavy-lidded amber eyes were not fixed on Diana's face. They were trained on the little gold key at Diana's throat.

There was a knock at the door.

Cassie started, hard enough that Laurel turned around and looked at her in surprise. But it was only Diana's father, who'd come home with a bulging briefcase in his hand.

Mr. Meade looked around the crowded room in mild surprise, as if he didn't quite know who all these people were. Cassie wondered suddenly how much he knew about the Circle.

"Is everyone staying for dinner?" he asked Diana.

"Oh—no," Diana said, looking at a dainty white and gold clock on the nightstand. "I didn't realize it was after seven, Dad. I'll fix something quick."

He nodded, and after one more quick, uncertain glance around the room, left.

Bedsprings creaked and clothing rustled as everyone else got up.

"Tomorrow we can meet at school," Melanie said. "But I've *got* to study tonight; this whole last week has been shot and I've got a biology test."

"Me too," said Laurel.

"I've got algebra homework," Suzan offered, and Deborah muttered, "Meaning you've got a week's worth of soap tapes in the VCR."

"All right, we'll meet tomorrow," Diana said. She walked downstairs with them. Faye managed to catch Cassie's arm as the others were leaving, and she breathed in her ear, "Get it tonight. Call me and I'll come and pick it up; then we'll put it back before morning so she won't notice it's gone."

Cassie pulled her arm away rebelliously. But at the door, Faye gave her a meaningful look, and the flash in those amber eyes alarmed her. She stared at Faye a long moment, then nodded slightly.

"Do you want me to stay?" Adam was saying to Diana.

"No," Cassie said quickly, before Diana could answer. They looked at her, startled, and she said, "I'll stay and help make dinner, if it's all right, Diana. I told my grandma and my mom I'd be gone and they've probably already eaten by now."

Diana's graciousness rose to the fore. "Oh— of course you can stay, then," she said. "We'll be fine, Adam."

"Okay." Adam gave Cassie a keen glance, which she returned woodenly. He went out, following Chris and Doug into the darkness. The flicker of a match up ahead showed where Nick was. Cassie looked up at the night sky, which glittered brashly with stars but not a trace of moon, and then stepped back as Diana shut the door.

Dinner was quiet, with Mr. Meade sitting there, leafing through a newspaper, occasionally glancing up over his reading glasses at the two girls. Afterward they went back up to Diana's room. Cassie realized she needed to stall.

"You know, you never told me about that print," she said, pointing. Decorating Diana's walls were six art prints. Five of them were very similar, black and white with a slightly old-fashioned look. Diana had told her they were pictures of Greek goddesses: Aphrodite, the beautiful but fickle goddess of love;

Artemis, the fierce virgin huntress; Hera, the imperious queen of the gods; Athena, the calm gray-eyed goddess of wisdom; and Persephone, who loved flowers and all growing things.

But the last print was different. It was in color, and the style was more abstract, more modern. It showed a young woman standing beneath a starry sky, while a crescent moon shone silver down on her flowing hair. She was wearing a simple white garment, cut high to show a garter on her thigh. On her upper arm was a silver cuff-bracelet, and on her head was a thin circlet with a crescent moon, horns upward.

It was the outfit Diana wore at meetings of the Circle.

"Who is she?" Cassie said, staring at the beautiful girl in the print.

"Diana," Diana said wryly. Cassie turned to her, and she smiled. "The goddess Diana," she added. "Not the Roman Diana; another one. She's older than all the Greek goddesses, and she was different from them. She was a Great Goddess; she ruled everything. She was goddess of the night and the moon and the stars—there's a story that once she turned all the stars into mice to impress the witches on earth. So they made her Queen of the Witches."

Cassie grinned. "I think it would take more than that to impress Faye."

"Probably. Some people say that her legend was based on an actual person, who taught magic and was a champion of poor women. Other people say she was first a Sun Goddess, but then she got chased out by male Sun Gods and turned to the night. The Romans got her confused with the Greek goddess Artemis—you know, the huntress—but she was much more than that. Anyway, she's always been Queen of the Witches."

"Like you," Cassie said.

Diana laughed and shook her head. "I may not *always* be leader," she said. "It all depends on what happens between now and November tenth. That's the day of the leadership vote."

"Why November tenth?"

"It's my birthday—Faye's too, coincidentally. You have to be seventeen to be permanent leader, and that's when we both will be."

Cassie was surprised. Diana was still only sixteen, like her? She always seemed so mature, and she was a senior. But it was even stranger that Faye was so young, and that the cousins had the same birthday.

She looked at Diana, sitting there on the bed. As beautiful as the girl in the last print was, Diana was more beautiful. With hair that indescribable color, like sunlight and moonlight woven together, and a face like a flower, and eyes like green jewels, Diana resembled something from a fairy tale or legend more than a real person. But the goodness and—well, *purity* that shone out of Diana's eyes were very real indeed, Cassie thought. Cassie was proud to be her friend.

Then the light flashed on the gold key around Diana's neck and she remembered what she was there to do.

I can't, Cassie thought, as her stomach plummeted giddily. She could feel the slow, sick pounding of her heart. Right this minute around her own neck was hanging the crescent-moon necklace that Diana had given her at her initiation. How could she steal from Diana, deceive Diana?

But she'd been through all that before. There was no way out. Faye would do exactly what she had threatened—Cassie knew that. The only way to save Diana was to deceive her.

It's for her own good, Cassie told herself. So

just stop thinking about it. Do what you have to and get it over with.

"Cassie? You look upset."

"I—" Cassie started to say, no, of course not, and change the subject the way she usually did when somebody caught her daydreaming. But then she had an idea. "I don't really feel like going home alone," she said, grimacing. "It's not just the walk—it's that house. It creaks and rattles all night long and sometimes I can't even get to sleep. Especially if I'm thinking about . . . about . . ."

"Is that all?" Diana said, smiling. "Well, that's easy to take care of. Sleep here." Cassie was stricken at how easily Diana made the offer. "And if you're worried about the skull," Diana went on, "you can stop. It's not going anywhere, and it's not going to do anything more to hurt people. I promise."

Cassie's face flamed and she had to struggle not to look at the cabinet. She would never have mentioned the skull herself: she couldn't have gotten the word out. "Okay," she said, trying to keep her voice normal. "Thanks. I'll call my mom and tell her I'm staying over."

"We can drive to your house so you can get dressed in the morning—I'll check on the guest room." As Diana left, the voices in Cassie's mind were rioting. *You little sneak*, they shouted at her. *You nasty, weaselly, lying little traitor—*

Shut up! Cassie shouted back at them, with such force that they actually did shut up.

She called her mother.

"The guest room's ready," Diana said, reappearing as Cassie hung up the phone. "But if you get scared in the night you can come in here."

"Thanks," Cassie said, genuinely grateful.

"What are big sisters for?"

They sat up and talked for a while, but neither of them had had much sleep the night before, and as the clock's hands edged closer to ten they were both yawning.

"I'll take my bath tonight so you can have one in the morning," Diana said. "The hot water doesn't last long around here."

"Isn't there a spell to take care of that?"

Diana laughed and tossed a book to her. "Here, see if you can find one."

It was the Book of Shadows Diana had brought to Cassie's initiation, the one that had been in Diana's family since the first witches came to New Salem. The brittle yellow pages had a mildewy smell that made Cassie wrinkle her nose, but she was glad to have this chance to look at it. Toward the beginning of the book the writing was small and almost illegible, but further on it became stylized and beautiful, like copperplate. Different authors, Cassie thought, different generations. The Post-it notes and plastic flags on almost every page were the work of the current generation.

It was full of spells, descriptions of coven meetings, rituals, and stories. Cassie pored over it, her eyes moving in fascination from one title to the next. Some of the spells seemed quaint and archaic; others were like something out of a modern pop-psychology book. Some were just timeless.

A Charm to Cure a Sickly Child, she read. *To Make Hens Lay. For Protection Against Fire and Water. To Overcome a Bad Habit. To Cast Out Fear and Malignant Emotions. To Find Treasure. To Change Your Luck. To Turn Aside Evil.*

A Talisman For Strength caught her eye.

Take a smooth and shapely rock, and upon one face carve the rising sun and a crescent moon, horns up. Upon the reverse, the words:

Strength of stone
Be in my bone

Power of light
Sustain my fight.

I could use that, Cassie thought. She continued flipping through the pages. A *Spell Against Contagious Disease*. *To Hold Evil Harmless*. *To Cause Dreams*.

And then, as if her guilty conscience had summoned it up, another spell appeared before her eyes. *For an Untrue Lover*.

Standing in the light of a full moon, take a strand of the lover's hair and tie knots in it, saying:

No peace find
No friend keep
No lover bind
No harvest reap

No repose take
No hunger feed
No thirst slake
No sorrow speed

No debt pay
No fear flee
Rue the day
You wronged me.

Cassie's pulse was fluttering in her wrists. Would anyone really put a curse like that on someone they loved, no matter how unfaithful?

She was still staring at the page when there was a movement at the door. She shut the book hastily as Diana came in, hair wrapped in a towel turban. But her eyes were drawn instantly to the gold chain Diana was dropping on the nightstand. It lay there next to a round stone with a spiral pattern in it, gray swirled with pale blue and sprinkled with quartz crystals. The chalcedony rose that Diana had given to Adam, and that Adam had given to Cassie. Now it was back where it belonged, Cassie thought, and something around her heart went numb.

"The bathroom's all yours," said Diana. "Here's a nightgown—or do you want a T-shirt?"

"A nightgown's fine," Cassie said. All the time she was washing up and changing she kept seeing the key. If only Diana would leave it there . . .

It was still on the nightstand when she popped her head back in Diana's room. Diana was already in bed.

"Want me to shut the door?"

"No," Diana said, reaching up to turn out the light. "Just leave it open a bit. Good night."

"Good night, Diana."

But once in the guest room next door Cassie propped herself up on two pillows and lay staring at the ceiling. Strangely, it was almost peaceful, lying there and knowing that for the moment there was nothing she could do but wait. She could hear the sound of the ocean behind Diana's house, now louder, now softer.

She waited a long time, listening to the quiet sounds. She felt relaxed, until she thought about getting up—then her heart started to pound.

At last she was sure Diana must be asleep. Now, she thought. If you don't move now, you never will.

Breath held, she shifted her weight in the bed and let her legs down. The hardwood floor creaked slightly as she crossed it, and she froze each time.

Outside Diana's door, she stood straining her ears. She could hear nothing. She put her hand on the door and slowly, by infinitesimal degrees, she pushed it open.

Carefully, lungs burning because she was afraid to breathe too loud, she placed one foot inside the threshold and let her weight down on it.

Diana was a dim shape on the bed. Please don't let her eyes be open, Cassie thought. She had the horrible fantasy that Diana was just lying there staring at her. But as she took another slow, careful step inside, and another, she could see that Diana's eyes were shut.

Oh, God, Cassie thought. I have to breathe. She opened her mouth and exhaled and inhaled silently. Her heart was shaking her and she felt dizzy.

Take tiny steps, she thought. She crept farther into the room until she was standing directly beside Diana.

On the nightstand, just a few inches from Diana's sleeping face, was the key.

Feeling as if she was moving in slow motion, Cassie put her hand out, placed it flat on the key. She didn't want to make any noise, but as she slid the necklace toward her, the chain rattled. She closed her fingers over it and held it tightly.

Now to get away. She forced herself to creep, all the time looking over her shoulder at the bed—was Diana waking up?

She reached the cabinet, and the little brass keyhole.

Fit the key in. She was fumbling; her fingers

felt clumsy as sausages. For a moment she panicked, thinking, what if it isn't the right key after all? But at last she got it in and turned it.

The lock clicked.

Hot relief swept over Cassie. She'd done it. Now she had to get the skull and call Faye—and what if Faye didn't answer? What if Diana's father caught her phoning in the middle of the night, or if Diana woke up and found the skull missing . . . ?

But as she eased the cabinet door open the world blurred and went dark before her eyes.

The hall light was shining into the cabinet. It was dim, but it was clear enough to show that all Cassie's caution had been in vain, and all her fears about getting the skull to Faye were pointless.

The cabinet was empty.

Cassie never knew how long she stood there, unable to think or move. But at last she pushed the cabinet door shut with shaking hands and locked it.

If it's not here, then *where* is it? Where? she demanded frantically of herself.

Don't think about it now. Put the key back. Or do you want her to wake up while you're standing here holding it?

The journey back to Diana's nightstand seemed to take forever, and her stomach ached as if someone were grinding a boot there. The key clinked as she replaced it on the nightstand and the chain stuck to her sweaty hand. But Diana's breathing remained soft and even.

Now get *out*, she ordered herself. She needed to be alone, to try and think. In her hurry to get away she forgot to be careful about placing her feet. A board creaked.

Just keep going, never mind, she thought. Then she heard something that stopped her heart.

A rustling from the bed. And then Diana's voice.

"Cassie?"

FOUR

"Cassie? Is that you?"

Sick dismay tingled down Cassie's nerves. Then she heard her own voice saying, as she turned, "I—I was scared . . . I didn't want to bother you . . ."

"Oh, don't be silly. Come lie down," Diana said sleepily, patting the bed beside her and shutting her eyes again.

It had worked. Cassie had gambled that Diana had just woken up that instant, and she'd been right. But Cassie felt as if she were reeling as she went over to the other side of the bed and got in, facing away from Diana.

"No more nightmares," Diana murmured.

"No," Cassie whispered. She could never get

up now and call Faye, but she didn't care. She was too tired of stress, of tension, of fear. And something deep inside her was glad that she hadn't been able to go through with it tonight. She shut her eyes and listened to the roaring in her own ears until she fell asleep.

In her dream she was on a ship. The deck was lifting and dropping beneath her, and waves rose up black over the sides. Lost, lost. . . What was lost? The ship? Yes, but something else, too. Lost forever . . . never find it now . . .

Then the dream changed. She was sitting in a bright and sunny room. Her chair was low to the ground, its spindly wood back so uncomfortable that she had to sit up straight. Her clothes were uncomfortable too; a bonnet as close-fitting as a swimming cap, and something tight around her waist that scarcely let her breathe. On her lap was a book.

Why, it was Diana's Book of Shadows! But no, the cover was different, red leather instead of brown. As she leafed through it, she saw that the writing in the beginning was very similar, and the titles of some of the spells were the same as in Diana's.

A *Charm to Cure a Sickly Child.* To *Make*

Hens Lay. For Protection Against Fire and Water. To Hold Evil Harmless.

To Hold Evil Harmless!

Her eyes moved swiftly across the words after it.

Bury the evil object in good moist loam or sand, well covered. The healing power of the Earth will battle with the poison, and if the object be not too corrupt, it will be purified.

Of course, Cassie thought. Of course.

The dream was ebbing. She could feel Diana's bed beneath her. But she could also hear a fading voice, calling a name. "Jacinth! Are you in there? Jacinth!"

Cassie was awake.

Diana's blue curtains were incandescent with the sunlight they held back. There were cheerful pottering noises in the room. But all Cassie could think about was the dream.

She must have read that spell in Diana's Book of Shadows last night, absorbed it unconsciously as she was flipping through. But why remember it in such a weird way?

It didn't matter. The problem was solved, and Cassie was so happy that she felt like hugging her pillow. Of course, of course!

Before the skull ceremony Diana had said the skull should be buried for purification—in moist sand. Adam had found it on the island buried in *sand*. Right below Diana's back door was a whole beach of sand. Cassie could hear the ocean breaking on it this minute.

The question was, could she find the exact *place* in the sand the skull was buried?

Faye was in writing class. And she was furious.

"I waited up all night," she hissed, grabbing Cassie by the arm. "What happened?"

"I couldn't get it. It wasn't there."

Faye's golden eyes narrowed and the long red-tipped fingers on Cassie's arm tightened. "You're lying."

"No," Cassie said. She cast an agonized glance around and then whispered, "I think I know where it is, but you have to give me time."

Faye was staring at her, those strange eyes raking hers. Then she relaxed slightly and smiled. "Of course, Cassie. All the time you need. Until Saturday."

"That may not be long enough—"

"It'll just have to be, won't it?" Faye drawled.

"Because after that I tell Diana." She let go and Cassie walked to her own desk. There was nothing else to do.

They had a minute of silence at the beginning of class for Mr. Fogle. Cassie spent the minute staring at her entwined fingers, thinking alternately of the dark rushing thing inside the skull and Doug Henderson's tip-tilted blue-green eyes.

At lunch there was a note taped on the glass door of the back room in the cafeteria. *Outside in front*, it said. Cassie turned from it and almost ran into Adam.

He was approaching with a loaded tray, and he lifted it to stop her from knocking it all over him.

"Whoa," he said.

Cassie flushed. But then, as they stood facing each other, she discovered a more serious problem. Adam's smile had faded, she couldn't stop flushing, and neither of them seemed to be going anywhere.

Eyes in the cafeteria were on them. Talk about déjà vu, Cassie thought. Every time I'm in here I'm the center of attention.

Finally, Adam made an abortive attempt to catch her elbow, stopped himself, and gestured her forward courteously. Cassie didn't know how he did it, but Adam managed to carry off courtesy like no guy she had ever known. It seemed to come naturally to him.

Girls looked up as they went by, some of them casting sideways glances at Adam. But these were different than the sideways glances Cassie had seen on the beach at Cape Cod. There, he'd been dressed in his scruffy fishing-boat clothes, and Portia's girlfriends had averted their eyes in disdain. These glances were shy, or inviting, or hopeful. Adam just tossed an unruly strand of red hair off his forehead and smiled at them.

Outside, the members of the Club were gathered on the steps. Even Nick was there. Cassie started toward them, and then a large shape bounded up and planted its front feet on her shoulders.

"Raj, get down! What are you doing?" Adam yelled.

A wet, warm tongue was lapping Cassie's face. She tried to fend the dog off, grabbing for the fur at the back of his neck, and ended it by hugging him.

"I think he's just saying 'hi,' " she gasped.

"He's usually so good about waiting just off

campus until I get out of school. I don't know why—" Adam broke off. "Raj, get down," he muttered in a changed voice. *"Now!"* he said, and snapped his fingers.

The lapping tongue withdrew, but the German shepherd stayed by Cassie's side as she walked over to the steps. She patted the dog's head.

"Raj usually hates new people," Sean observed as Cassie and Adam sat down. "So how come he always likes you so much?"

Cassie could feel Faye's mocking eyes on her and she shrugged uncomfortably, staring down into her lunch sack. Then something occurred to her: one of those witty comebacks she usually only thought of the next day.

"Must be my new perfume. Eau de pot roast," she said, and Laurel and Diana giggled. Even Suzan smirked.

"All right, let's get down to business," Diana said then. "I brought us out here to make sure nobody's listening. Anybody have any new ideas?"

"Any one of us *could* have done it," Melanie said quietly.

"Only *some* of us had any reason to," Adam replied.

"Why?" said Laurel. "I mean, just because Mr. Fogle was obnoxious wasn't a reason to murder him. And quit grinning like that, Doug, unless you really did do something."

"Maybe Fogle knew too much," Suzan said unexpectedly. Everyone turned to her, but she went on unwrapping a Hostess cupcake without looking up.

"So?" said Deborah at last. "What's that supposed to mean?"

"Well . . ." Suzan raised china-blue eyes to look around at the group. "Fogle always got here at the crack of dawn, didn't he? And his office is right up there, isn't it?" She nodded, and Cassie followed her gaze to a window on the second floor of the red-brick building. Then Cassie looked down the hill, to the bottom where Kori had been found.

There was a pause, and then Diana said, "Oh, my God."

"What?" Chris demanded, looking around. Deborah scowled and Laurel blinked. Faye was chuckling.

"She's saying he might have seen Kori's murderer," Adam said. "And then whoever killed her, killed him to keep him from talking. But do we *know* he was here that morning?"

Cassie was now staring from the second-story window to the chimney that rose from the school. It had been cold the morning they found Kori dead, and the principal had a fireplace in his office. Had there been smoke rising from the chimney that morning?

"You know," she said softly to Diana, "I think he *was* here."

"Then that could be it," Laurel said excitedly. "And it would mean it couldn't have been one of us who killed him—because whoever killed him killed Kori, too. And none of us would have done *that*."

Diana was looking vastly relieved, and there were nods around the Circle. A little voice inside Cassie was trying to say something, but she pushed it down.

Nick, however, had his lip curled. "And who besides one of us would have been able to drop an avalanche on somebody?"

"Anybody with a stick or a crowbar," Deborah snapped. "Those rocks on the cliff at Devil's Cove are just piled up any old way. An outsider could've done it easy. So it's back to the question of which of them did it—if we have to ask anymore." There was a hunting light in her face, and Chris and Doug were looking eager.

"You leave Sally alone until we figure this out," Diana said flatly.

"And Jeffrey," Faye added throatily, with a meaningful look. Deborah glared at her, then at last dropped her eyes.

"Now that we've got *that* solved, I have a real problem to talk about," Suzan said, brushing crumbs off the front of her sweater, an interesting process which Sean and the Hendersons watched avidly. "Homecoming is in less than two weeks, and I haven't figured out who to ask yet. And I haven't even got any *shoes* . . ."

The meeting degenerated, and shortly after that the bell rang.

"Who are you going to ask to Homecoming?" Laurel asked Cassie that afternoon. They were driving home from school with Diana and Melanie.

"Oh . . ." Cassie was taken aback. "I haven't thought about it. I—I've never asked a guy to a dance in my life."

"Well, now's the time to start," Melanie said. "Usually the outsiders don't ask us—they're a little scared. But you can have any guy you want; just pick him and tell him to show up."

"Just like that?"

"Yep," Laurel said cheerfully. "Like that. Of course, Melanie and I don't usually ask guys who're together with somebody. But Faye and Suzan . . ." She rolled her eyes. "They *like* picking guys who're taken."

"I've noticed," Cassie said. There was no question about whom Diana went to dances with. "What about Deborah?"

"Oh, Deb usually just goes stag," said Laurel. "She and the Hendersons hang out, playing cards and stuff in the boiler room. And Sean just goes from girl to girl to girl; none of them like him, but they're all too scared not to dance with him. You'll see it there; it's funny."

"I probably won't see it," Cassie said. The idea of walking up to some guy and ordering him to escort her was simply unthinkable. Impossible, even if she was a witch. She might as well tell everybody now and let them get used to it. "I probably won't go. I don't like dances much."

"But you *have* to go," Laurel said, dismayed, and Diana said, "It's the most fun—really, Cassie. Look, let's go to my house right now and talk about guys you can ask."

"No, I've got to go straight home," Cassie said quickly. She had to go home because she had to look for the skull. Faye's words had been ringing in the back of her mind all day, and now they drowned out Diana's voice. *All the time you need—until Saturday.* "Please just drop me off at my house."

In silence that was bewildered and a little hurt, Diana complied.

All that week, Cassie looked for the skull.

She looked on the beach where her initiation had been held, where stumps of candles and pools of melted wax could still be seen half buried in the sand. She looked on the beach below Diana's house, among the eelgrass and driftwood. She looked up and down the bluffs, walking on the dunes each afternoon and evening. It made sense that Diana would have marked the place somehow, but with what kind of mark? Any bit of flotsam or jetsam on the sand could be it.

As each day went by she got more and more worried. She'd been so sure she could find it; it was just a matter of *looking.* But now it seemed she'd looked at every inch of beach for miles, and all she'd found was sea wrack and a few old beer bottles.

On Saturday morning she stepped out of the front door to see a bright-red car circling in the cul-de-sac a little past her grandmother's house. There was no building at the very point of the headland where the road dead-ended, but the car was circling there. As Cassie stood in the doorway, it turned and cruised slowly by her house. It was Faye's Corvette ZR1, and Faye was in it, one languid arm drooping out of the window.

As she went by Cassie, Faye raised her hand and held up one finger, its long nail gleaming even redder than the car's paint job. Then she turned and mouthed a single word at Cassie.

Sunset.

She went cruising on without a backward look. Cassie stared after her.

Cassie knew what she meant. By sunset, either Cassie brought the skull to Faye, or Faye told Diana.

I *have* to find it, Cassie thought. I don't care if I have to sift through every square inch of sand from here to the mainland. I have to *find* it.

But that day was just like the others. She crawled on her knees over the beach near the initiation site, getting sand inside her jeans, in her shoes. She found nothing.

The ocean rolled and roared beside her, the smell of salt and decaying seaweed filled her nostrils. As the sun slipped farther and farther down in the west, the crescent moon over the ocean glowed brighter. Cassie was exhausted and terrified, and she was giving up hope.

Then, as the sky was darkening, she saw the ring of stones.

She'd passed by them a dozen times before. They were bonfire stones, stained black with charcoal. But what were they doing so close to the waterline? At high tide, Cassie thought, they'd be covered. She knelt beside them and touched the sand in their center.

Moist.

With fingers that trembled slightly, she dug there. Dug deeper and deeper until her fingertips touched something hard.

She dug around it, feeling the curve of its shape, until she had loosened enough sand to lift it out. It was shockingly heavy and covered with a thin white cloth. Cassie didn't need to remove the cloth to know what it was.

She felt like hugging it.

She'd done it! She'd found the skull, and

now she could take it to Faye. . . .

The feeling of triumph died inside her. Faye. Could she really take the skull to Faye?

All the time she'd been looking for it, *finding* it hadn't been real to her. She hadn't thought further than simply getting her hands on it.

Now that she was actually holding it, now that the possibility was before her . . . she couldn't do it.

The thought of those hooded golden eyes examining it, of those fingers with their long red nails gripping it, made Cassie feel sick. An image flitted through her mind, of a golden-eyed falcon with its talons extended. A bird of prey.

She couldn't go through with it.

But then what about Diana? Cassie's head bent in exhaustion, in defeat. She didn't know what to do about Diana. She didn't know how to solve anything. All she knew was that she couldn't hand the skull over to Faye.

There was a throat-clearing sound behind her.

"I knew you could do it," Faye said in her husky voice as Cassie, still on her knees, spun around to look. "I had complete faith in you, Cassie. And now my faith is justified."

"How did you know?" Cassie was on her feet. "How did you know where I was?"

Faye smiled. "I told you I have friends who see a lot. One of them just brought me the news."

"It doesn't matter," Cassie said, forcibly calming herself. "You can't have it, Faye."

"That's where you're wrong. I *do* have it. I'm stronger than you are, Cassie," Faye said. And as she stood there on a little dune above Cassie, tall and stunning in black pants and a loose-knit scarlet top, Cassie knew it was true. "I'm taking the skull now. You can run to Diana if you want, but you'll be too late."

Cassie stared at her a long minute, breathing quickly. Then she said, "No. I'm coming with you."

"What?"

"I'm coming with you." In contrast to Faye, Cassie was small. And she was dirty and disheveled, with sand in every crease of her clothes and under her fingernails, but she was relentless. "You said you only wanted the skull to 'look at it for a while.' That was the reason I agreed to get it for you. Well, now I've found it, but I'm not going to leave you alone with it. I'm going with you. I want to watch."

Faye's black eyebrows, curved like a raven's wings, lifted higher. "So voyeurism's your idea of fun."

"No, it's yours—or your *friends'*, rather," Cassie said.

Faye chuckled. "You're not such a spineless mouse after all, are you?" she said. "All right; come. You might find it's more fun to join in than to watch, anyway."

Faye shut the bedroom door behind Cassie. Then she went and took something out of the closet. It was a comforter, not rose-patterned like the one on the bed, but red satin.

"My spare," Faye said, with an arch smile. "For special occasions." She shook it out over the bed, then went around the room lighting candles that gave off pungent, heady scents. Then she opened a velvet-lined box.

Cassie stared. Inside was a jumble of loose stones, some polished, some uncut. They were dark green and amethyst, black, sulfur-yellow, pale pink and cloudy orange.

"Find the red ones," Faye said.

Cassie's fingers were itching to get into them anyway. She began to sort through the rainbow clutter.

"Those garnets are good," Faye said, approving some burgundy-colored stones. "And carnelians, too, if they're not too orange. Now let me see: fire opal for passion, red jasper for stability. And one black onyx for surrendering to your shadow self." She smiled strangely at Cassie, who stiffened.

Undisturbed, Faye arranged the stones in a circle on the comforter. Then she turned off the lamp and the room was lit only by the candles.

"Now," Faye said, "for our guest."

Cassie thought that was an odd way to put it, and there was a sinking in her stomach as Faye opened the backpack. She'd promised herself that she would keep Faye from doing anything too terrible with the skull—but how?

"Just what are you planning to do with it?" she asked, trying to keep her voice steady.

"Just scrying," murmured Faye, but she wasn't paying much attention to Cassie. She was gazing down as she slowly peeled the wet, sandy white cloth away to reveal the glittering dome of the crystal skull. As Cassie watched, Faye lifted the skull up to eye level, cradling it in red-tipped fingers. Reflections of the candle flames danced in the depths of the crystal.

"Ah," said Faye. "Hello there." She was gazing into the empty eyesockets as if looking at a lover. She bent forward and lightly kissed the grinning quartz teeth.

Then she put the skull in the center of the ring of gems.

Cassie swallowed. The sinking feeling was getting worse and worse; she felt sicker and sicker. "Faye, shouldn't you have a ring of candles, too? What if—"

"Don't be silly. Nothing's going to happen. I just want to see what this fellow's all about," Faye murmured.

Cassie didn't believe it.

"Faye . . ." She was starting to panic. This was a bad idea, this had always been a bad idea. She wasn't strong enough to stop Faye from anything. She didn't even know what Faye was *doing*.

"Faye, don't you need to prepare—"

"Be quiet," Faye said sharply. She was hovering over the skull, gazing down into it, half reclining on the bed.

It was all happening too fast. And it wasn't safe. Cassie felt sure of that now. She could feel a darkness welling up inside the skull.

"Faye, what are you *doing* with it?"

More darkness, rising up like the sea. How could Faye be this powerful, to raise it from the skull so quickly? And all by herself, without a coven to back her up?

The star ruby at Faye's throat winked, and for the first time Cassie noticed matching gems on Faye's fingers. All these red stones—to heighten the energy of the ritual? To enhance the power of the witch—or the skull?

"Faye!"

"Shut up!" said Faye. She leaned farther over the skull, lips parted, her breath coming quickly. Cassie could almost see the darkness in the skull, swirling, rising like smoke.

Don't look at it! Don't give it any more power! the voice in her head cried. Cassie stared instead at Faye, urgently.

"Faye, whatever you're doing—it's not what you think! It's not safe!"

"Leave me *alone*!"

Swirling, rising, higher and higher. The darkness had been thin and transparent at first, but now it was thick and oily. Cassie wouldn't look at it, but she could feel it. It was almost at the top of the skull, uncoiling, wheeling.

"Faye, look out!"

The black-haired girl was directly over the

skull, directly in the way of the rising dark. Cassie grabbed her, pulling at her.

But Faye was strong. Snarling something incoherent, she tried to shake Cassie off. Cassie threw one glance at the skull. It seemed to be grinning wildly at her, the smoke corkscrewing inside it.

"*Faye*," she screamed, and wrenched at the other girl's shoulders.

They both fell backward. At the same instant, out of the corner of her eye, Cassie saw the darkness break free.

FIVE

"You stupid *outsider*," Faye screeched, twisting away from Cassie. "It was just getting started—now you've ruined everything!"

Cassie lay on her back, gasping. Then she pointed shakily, sitting up.

"That's what I ruined," she said, her voice soft from lack of breath, and from fear. Faye looked up at the ceiling, at the dark, charred circle on the white plaster.

"It was coming right at you," Cassie said, too unnerved to yell, or even to be angry. "Didn't you *see* it?"

Faye just looked at her, black lashes heavy over speculative golden eyes. Then she looked at the skull.

Cassie leaned over and covered the skull with the cloth.

"What are you doing?"

"I'm taking it back," Cassie said, still breathless. "Diana was right. *I* was right, if I'd listened to myself. It's too dangerous to handle."

She expected Faye to explode, possibly even to fight her. But Faye looked up at the stain on the ceiling and said musingly, "I think it's just a matter of more protection. If we could capture that energy—channel it . . ."

"You're crazy," Cassie told her bluntly. "And," she added, "our deal is finished. I did what you asked: I brought you the skull. You used it and you almost got killed. So now it's over."

Faye's lazy expression disappeared. "Oh, no, Cassie," she said. The hint of a smile curved her lips, but her eyes were predatory. Ruthless. "It's only starting. Don't you see?" She began to laugh. "You're more my captive now than ever. It's not just Adam anymore—now I can tell Diana about *this*. How do you think the Princess of Purity is going to feel when she finds out her 'little sister' stole the skull? And then brought it to *me* to use?" Faye laughed harder, seeming delighted. "Oh, Cassie, you should see your face."

Cassie felt as if she were smothering. What Faye said was true. If Diana found out that Cassie had dug up the skull—that Cassie had lied to her—that the whole story last Sunday about being too scared to go home had been a trick . . .

Just as it had the last time she'd stood in this room, Cassie felt her spirit, her will, draining away. She was more trapped than ever. She was lost.

"You take the skull back now," Faye said, as if it had been entirely her idea. "And later— well, I'll think of something else I want from you. In the meanwhile, you just keep yourself available."

I hate you, Cassie thought with impotent rage. But Faye was ignoring Cassie completely, bending to pick up the bristling kittens, one gray and one orange, which had crawled out from under the dust ruffle. The vampire kittens, Cassie remembered distractedly—the ones with a taste for human blood. Apparently even *they* hadn't liked this business with the skull.

"What about that?" Cassie said, pointing at

the dark stain on Faye's ceiling. "Don't you feel at all responsible about letting it loose? It could be out killing somebody—"

"I doubt it," Faye said, and shrugged negligently. "But we'll just have to wait and see, I suppose." She stroked the orange kitten and its fur began to lie flat again.

Cassie could only stare at her, tears rising to her eyes. She'd thought she could control Faye, but she'd been wrong. And right now the new dark energy could be doing anything, and she was helpless to stop it.

You could tell Diana, an inner voice, the core voice, whispered, but Cassie didn't even pretend to listen. She could never tell Diana now; that chance was over. Things had gone far too far with Faye.

"Cassie, are you nervous about something?" Laurel had paused with the white-handled knife in her hand.

"Me? No. Why?" Cassie said, feeling every moment as if she might jump out of her skin.

"You just seem kind of jittery." Laurel gently snicked the knife through the base of the small witch-hazel bush. "Now, this won't hurt a bit . . . you've got plenty of roots down there to grow

73

back from . . ." she murmured soothingly. "It's not about Homecoming, is it?" she asked, looking up again.

"No, no," Cassie said. She hadn't even thought about Homecoming this week. She couldn't think about anything except the dark energy. Each day she expected to hear about some new disaster.

But today was Thursday, and nothing had happened yet. No avalanches, no bodies found, nobody even missing. Oh, if only she could let herself believe that nothing *would* happen. The energy she and Faye had released had been small—she felt sure of that now—and maybe it had just evaporated. Cassie felt a delicious peace steal through her at the thought.

Laurel had moved over to a clump of thyme. "It's not too late to change your mind about coming," she said. "And I wish you would. Dancing is very witchy—and it's *Nature*. It's like one of our incantations:

"Man to woman, woman to man,
Ever since the world began.
Heart to heart, and hand to hand,
Ever since the world began."

She added, looking up at Cassie thoughtfully, "Wasn't there some guy you met over the summer that you were interested in? We could do a spell to pull him here—"

"No!" said Cassie. "I mean, I really don't want to go to Homecoming, Laurel. I just—I wouldn't be comfortable."

"Thank you," Laurel said. For an instant Cassie thought it was addressed to her, but Laurel was now talking to the thyme. "I'm sorry I needed part of the root, too, but I brought this to help you grow back," she went on, tucking a pink crystal into the soil. "That reminds me, have you found your working crystal yet?" she said to Cassie.

"No," Cassie said. She thought of the jumble of crystals in Faye's box. She'd liked handling them, but none of them had stood out as *hers*, as the one she needed as a witch.

"Don't worry, you will," Laurel assured her. "It'll just turn up one day, and you'll *know*." She stood up with the thyme plant in her hand. "All right, let's go inside and I'll show you how to make an infusion. Nobody should fool around with herbs unless they know exactly what they're doing. And if you change your mind about Homecoming, thyme soup helps overcome shyness."

Cassie cast a look around the great wide

world, as she always did now, checking for the dark energy, then she followed Laurel.

The next day, in American history class, Diana sneezed.

Ms. Lanning stopped talking and said, "Bless you" absently. Cassie scarcely noticed it at the time. But then, at the end of class, Diana sneezed again, and kept sneezing. Cassie looked at her. Diana's eyes were pink and watery. Her nose was getting pink, too, as she rubbed it with a Kleenex.

That night, instead of going to the Homecoming game, Diana stayed at home in bed. Cassie, who knew nothing about football and was only yelling when everybody else yelled, worried about her in some back corner of her mind. It *couldn't* have anything to do with the dark energy, could it?

"Applaud," Laurel said, nudging her. "For the Homecoming Queen. Sally really looks almost pretty, doesn't she?"

"I guess," Cassie said, applauding mechanically. "Laurel, how come one of *us* isn't Homecoming Queen? Instead of an outsider?"

"Diana didn't want to be," Laurel said succinctly. "And Deb and the others think it's too goody-goody. But from the way Jeffrey Lovejoy's looking at Sally, I'd say Faye made a mistake. She told Jeff to come to the dance with her, but he'd already asked Sally and he's a fighter. It'll be interesting to see who gets him."

"You can tell me all about it," Cassie said. "I saw the last fight between Faye and Sally; this one I can miss."

But it didn't turn out that way.

Cassie was in the herb garden when the phone call came. She had to go through the kitchen and into the new wing of the house to get to the telephone.

"Hello, Cassie?" The voice was so muted and stuffed-up it was almost unrecognizable. "It's Diana."

Fear crinkled up Cassie's backbone. The dark energy . . . "Oh, Diana, are you *all right?*"

There was a burst of muffled laughter. "Don't panic. I'm not dying. It's just a bad cold."

"You sound awful."

"I know. I'm completely miserable, and I can't go to the dance tonight, and I called to ask you a favor."

Cassie froze with a sudden intuition. Her

mouth opened, and then shut again silently. But Diana was going on.

"Jeffrey called Faye to tell her he's going with Sally after all, and Faye is *livid*. So when she heard I was sick, she called to say she would go with Adam, because she knew I would want him to go even if I couldn't. And I do; I don't want him to miss it just because of me. So I told her she couldn't because I'd already asked you to go with him."

"*Why?*" Cassie blurted, and then thought, Ask a stupid question . . .

"Because Faye is on the prowl," Diana said patiently. "And she likes Adam, and the mood she's in tonight, she'll try anything. That's the one thing I couldn't stand, Cassie, for her to get her hands on Adam. I just couldn't."

Cassie looked around for something to sit down on.

"But Diana . . . I don't even have a dress. I'm all *muddy*. . . ."

"You can go over to Suzan's. All the other girls are there. They'll take care of you."

"But . . ." Cassie shut her eyes. "Diana, you just don't understand. I *can't*. I—"

"Oh, Cassie, I know it's a lot to ask. But I don't know who else to turn to. And if Faye goes after Adam . . ."

It was the first time Cassie had ever heard such a forlorn note in Diana's voice. She sounded on the verge of tears. Cassie pressed a hand to her forehead. "Okay. Okay, I'll do it. But—"

"Thank you, Cassie! Now go right to Suzan's—I've talked with her and Laurel and Melanie. They'll fix you up. I'm going to call Adam and tell him."

And *that*, Cassie thought helplessly, was one conversation she thought she could miss too.

Maybe Adam would get them out of it somehow, she thought as she drove the Rabbit up Suzan's driveway. But she doubted it. When Diana made her mind up about something, she was immovable.

Suzan's house had columns. Cassie's mother said it was bad Greek Revival, but Cassie secretly thought it was impressive. The inside was imposing too, and Suzan's bedroom was in a class by itself.

It was all the colors of the sea: sand, shell, pearl, periwinkle. The headboard on Suzan's bed was shaped like a giant scalloped shell. But what caught Cassie's eye were the mirrors—she'd never seen so many mirrors in one place.

"Cassie!" Laurel burst in just behind her, making Cassie turn in surprise. "I've got it!" Laurel announced triumphantly to the other girls, holding up a plastic-draped hanger. Inside Cassie glimpsed some pale, gleaming material.

"It's a dress Granny Quincey got me this summer—but I haven't worn it and I never will. It's not my style, but it'll be perfect on you, Cassie."

"Oh, God," was all Cassie could think of to say. She'd changed her mind; she couldn't do this after all. "Laurel—thanks—but I might ruin it . . ."

"Don't let her talk," Melanie ordered from the other side of the room. "Stick her in a bath; she needs one."

"That way," Suzan said, gesturing with splayed fingers. "I can't do anything until my nails are dry, but all the stuff's in there."

"Beauty bath mix," Laurel gloated, examining the assortment of bottles on the gilt shelves in Suzan's bathroom. There were all kinds of bottles, some with wide necks and some with long narrow necks, green and deep glowing blue. "Here, this is great: thyme, mint, rosemary, and lavender. It smells wonderful, and it's tranquilizing, too." She scattered bright-colored dried flowers in the steaming water. "Now get in and scrub. Oh, *this* is good," she went on, sniffing at another bottle. "Chamomile hair rinse—it brightens hair, brings out the highlights. Use it!"

Cassie obeyed dazedly. She felt as if she'd just been inducted into boot camp.

When she got back to the bedroom, Melanie directed her to sit down and hold a hot washcloth on her face. "It's 'a fragrant resin redolent with the mysterious virtues of tropical balms,' " Melanie said, reading from a Book of Shadows. "It 'renders the complexion clear and brilliant'—and it really does, too. So hold this on your face while I do your hair."

"Melanie's wonderful with hair," Laurel volunteered as Cassie gamely buried her face in the washcloth.

"Yes, but I'm not going to give her a *do*," Melanie said critically. "I'm just making it soft and natural, waving back from her face. Plug in those hot rollers, Suzan."

While Melanie worked, Cassie could hear Laurel and Deborah arguing in the depths of Suzan's walk-in closet.

"Suzan," Laurel shouted. "I never saw so

many pairs of shoes in my life. What do you *do* with them all?"

"I don't know. I just like buying them. Which is lucky for people who want to borrow them," Suzan called back.

"Now, let's get you into the dress," Melanie said, some time later. "No, don't look, not yet. Come over to the vanity and Suzan will do your makeup."

Feebly, Cassie tried to protest as Melanie whipped a towel around her neck. "That's all right. I can do it myself—"

"No, you *want* Suzan to do it," Laurel said, emerging from the closet. "I promise, Cassie; just wait and see."

"But I don't wear much makeup—i won't look like me . . ."

"Yes, you will. You'll look more like you."

"Well, somebody decide, for heaven's sake," Suzan said, standing by in a kimono and waving a powder puff impatiently. "I've got myself to do, too, you know."

Cassie yielded and sat on a stool, facing Suzan. "Hm," said Suzan, turning Cassie's face this way and that. "Hmm."

The next half hour was filled with bewildering instructions. "Look up," Suzan commanded, wielding a brown eyeliner pencil. "Look down. See, this will give you doe eyes," she went on, "and nobody will even be able to tell you're wearing anything. Now a little almond shadow . . ." She dipped a small brush in powder and blew off the excess. "Now just a little midnight blue in the crease to make you look mysterious . . ."

Eyes shut, Cassie relaxed. This was fun. She felt even more decadent and pampered when Laurel said, "I'll take care of your nails."

"What are you using?" Cassie asked trustingly.

"Witch-hazel infusion and Chanel Flamme Rose polish," Laurel replied, and they both giggled.

"Don't jolt my hand," Suzan said crossly. "Now suck in your cheeks like a fish. Stop laughing. You've got great cheekbones, I'm just going to bring them out a little. Now go like this; I'm going to put Roseglow on your lips."

When at last she sat back to survey her work, the other girls gathered around, even Deborah.

"And finally," Suzan said, "just a *drop* of magnet perfume here, and here, and here." She touched the hollow of Cassie's throat, her earlobes, and her wrists with something that smelled wild and exotic and wonderful.

"What is it?" Cassie asked.

"Mignonette, tuberose, and ylang-ylang," Suzan said. "It makes you irresistible. And I should know."

Alarm lanced through Cassie suddenly, but before she had time to think, Laurel was turning her, loosening the towel around her neck. "Wait, don't look until you've got your shoes on. . . . Now!" Laurel said jubilantly. "Look at that!"

Cassie opened her eyes and drew in her breath. Then, scarcely knowing what she was doing, she moved closer to the full-length mirror, to the lovely stranger reflected there. She could hardly resist reaching out to touch the glass with her fingertips.

The girl in the mirror had fine, light-brown hair waving softly back from her face. The highlights shimmered when Cassie moved her head, so it must be her—but it *couldn't* be, Cassie thought. *Her* eyes didn't have that dreamy, mysterious aura. Her skin didn't have that dewy glow, and she didn't blush that way, to bring out her cheekbones. And her lips definitely didn't have that breathless ready-to-be-kissed look.

"It's the lipstick," Suzan explained. "Don't smudge it."

"It's possible," said Melanie, "that you've gone too far, Suzan."

"Do you like the dress?" Laurel asked. "It's the perfect length, just short enough, but still romantic."

The girl in the mirror, the one with the delicate bones and the swan's neck, turned from side to side. The dress was silvery and shimmering, like yards of starlight, and it made Cassie feel like a princess. Suzan's shoes, appropriately, looked like glass slippers.

"Oh, thank you!" Cassie said, whirling to look at the other girls. "I mean—I don't know how to say thank you. I mean—I finally look like a witch!"

They burst into laughter, except Deborah, who threw a disgusted glance at the ceiling. Cassie hugged Laurel, and then, impulsively, hugged Suzan, too.

"Well, you are a witch," Suzan said reasonably. "I'll show you how to do it yourself if you want."

Cassie felt something like humility. She'd thought Suzan was just an airhead, but it wasn't true. Suzan loved beauty and was generous about sharing it with other people. Cassie smiled into the china-blue eyes and felt as if she'd unexpectedly made a new friend.

"Wait, we almost forgot!" Melanie said. "You can't go to a dance without a single crystal to your name." She rummaged in her canvas bag, and then said, "Here, this will be perfect; it was my great-grandmother's." She held up a necklace: a thin chain with a teardrop of clear quartz. Cassie took it lovingly and fastened it around her neck, admiring the way it lay in the hollow of her throat. Then she hugged Melanie, too.

From downstairs a doorbell chimed faintly, and, closer, a male voice shouted, "For crying out loud! Are you going to get that, Suzan?"

"It's one of the guys!" Suzan said, thrown into a tizzy. "And we're not ready. You're the only one dressed, Cassie; run and get it before Dad has a fit."

"Hello, Mr. Whittier; sorry, Mr. Whittier," Cassie gasped as she hurried downstairs. It wasn't until she was at the door that she thought, Oh, please, please, please, let it be any one of the others. Don't let it be *him*. Please.

Adam was standing there when she opened the door.

He was wearing a wry smile, appropriate for a guy who's been commandeered at the last minute into escorting his girl's best friend to a dance. The smile disappeared instantly when he saw Cassie.

For a long moment he simply stared at her. Her own elated smile faded, and they stood gazing at each other.

Adam swallowed hard, started to say something, then gave up and stood silent again.

Cassie was hearing Suzan's words: *It'll make you irresistible*. Oh, what had she done?

"We'll call it off," she said, and her voice was as soft as when she'd told Faye about the dark energy. "We'll tell Diana I got sick too—"

"We can't," he said, equally soft, but very intense. "Nobody would believe it, and besides . . ." The wry smile made an attempt at reappearing. "It would be a shame for you to miss Homecoming. You look . . ." He paused. "Nice."

"So do you," Cassie said, and tried to come up with an ironic smile of her own. She had the feeling it turned out wobbly.

Cassie took another breath, but at that moment she heard a voice from the second floor.

"Here," Laurel said, leaning over the balustrade to toss Cassie a tiny beaded purse. "Get her to the dance, Adam; that way she'll have a chance at some guys who're available." And, from the bedroom, Suzan called, "But not too many, Cassie—leave some for us!"

"I'll try to fend a few of them off," Adam called back, and Cassie felt her racing pulse calm a little. They had their parts down now. It was like acting in a play, and all Cassie had to do was remember her role. She felt sure Adam could handle his . . . well, almost sure. Something in his sea-dark eyes sent thin chills up her spine.

"Let's go," Adam said, and Cassie took a deep breath and stepped with him outside into the night.

SIX

They drove to the school. Despite the tension between them, the night seemed clear and cool and filled with magic, and the gym was transformed. It was so big that it seemed part of the night, and the twinkling lights woven around the pipes and girders overhead were like stars.

Cassie looked around for any other members of the Circle. She didn't see any. What she saw were outsiders looking in surprise at her and Adam. And in the boys' eyes there was something more than surprise, something Cassie wasn't at all used to. It was the kind of open-mouthed stare guys turned on Diana when Diana was looking particularly beautiful.

A sudden warmth and a glow that had nothing to do with Suzan's artistry swept over Cassie. She knew she was blushing. She felt conspicuous and overwhelmed—and at the same time thrilled and excited. But through the wild mixture of emotions, one thing remained clear and diamond-bright within her. She was here to play a part and to keep her oath to be true to Diana. That was what mattered, and she clung to it.

But she couldn't just stand here with everyone staring at her any longer; it was too embarrassing. She turned to Adam.

It was an awkward moment. They couldn't sit down together in some dark corner—that would never do. Then Adam gave a crooked smile and said, "Want to dance?"

Relieved, Cassie nodded, and they went out onto the dance floor. In a matter of seconds they were surrounded by other people.

And then the music started, soft and sweet.

They stared at each other, helplessly, in dismay. They were in the middle of the dance floor; to get out they would have to forge their way through the crowd. Cassie looked into Adam's eyes and saw he was as confused as she was.

Then Adam said under his breath, "We'd better not be too conspicuous," and he took her in his arms.

Cassie shut her eyes. She was trembling, and she didn't know what to do.

Slowly, almost as if compelled, Adam laid his cheek against her hair.

I won't think about anything, I won't think at all, Cassie told herself. I won't *feel* . . . But that was impossible. She couldn't help feeling. It was dark as twilight and Adam was holding her and she could smell his scent of autumn leaves and ocean wind.

Dancing is a very witchy thing—oh, Laurel had been right. Cassie could imagine witches in ages past dancing under the stars to wild sweet music, and then lying down on the soft green grass.

Maybe among Cassie's ancestors there had been some witch-girl who had danced like this in a moonlit glade. Maybe she had danced by herself until she noticed a shadow among the trees and heard the panpipes. And then maybe she and the forest god had danced together, while the moon shone silver all around them. . . .

Cassie could feel the warmth, the course of life, in Adam's arms. The silver cord, she thought. The mysterious, invisible bond that had connected her to Adam from the beginning . . . just now she could feel it again. It joined them heart to heart, it was drawing them irresistibly together.

The music stopped. Adam moved back just slightly and she looked up at him, cheek and neck tingling with the loss of his warmth. His eyes were strange, darkness just edged with silver like a new moon. Slowly, he bent down so that his lips were barely touching hers—and stayed there. They stood that way for what seemed like an eternity and then Cassie turned her head away.

It wasn't a kiss, she thought as they moved out through the crowd. It didn't count. But there was no way that they could dance together again and they both knew it. Cassie's knees were shaking.

Find some people to join—fast, she thought. She looked around desperately. And to her vast relief she glimpsed a sleek auburn crop and a head of long, light-brown hair interwoven with tiny flowers. It was Melanie and Laurel, in animated conversation with two outsider boys. If they'd seen what happened on the dance floor a minute ago . . .

But Laurel swung around at Adam's "hello" and said, "Oh, there you are!" and Melanie's smile was quite normal. Cassie was grateful to talk with them while the boys talked about football. Her lightheartedness, inspired by the magic of the dance, began to return.

"There's Deborah. She always gets one dance in before heading off to the boiler room with the Hendersons," Laurel murmured, smiling mischievously.

"What do they *do* there?" Cassie asked as she followed Laurel's gaze. Deborah was wearing a black micro-mini and a biker's hat decorated with a gold link bracelet. Her hair was mostly in her eyes. She looked great.

"Play cards and drink. But no, not what you're thinking. None of the guys would dare try anything with Deb—she can outwrestle them all. They're just in awe of her."

Cassie smiled, then she spotted someone else, and her smile faded. "Speaking of awesome . . ." she said softly.

Faye had on a flame-colored dress, sexy and elegant, cut in her usual knockout style. Her hair was black and glossy, hanging untamed down her back. She was like some exotic creature that had wandered onto campus by accident.

Faye didn't see the three girls scrutinizing her. Her entire attention seemed to be focused on Nick.

Cassie was surprised Nick was even here; he wasn't the type to go to dances. He was standing by a blond outsider girl who looked frankly spooked. As Cassie watched, Faye made her way over to him and placed a hand with red-tipped fingers on his arm.

Nick glanced down at the hand and stiffened. He threw a cold glance over his shoulder at Faye. Then, deliberately, he shrugged her hand off, bending over the little blonde, whose eyes widened. Throughout the whole incident his face remained as wintry and remote as ever.

"Uh-oh," Laurel whispered. "Faye's trying to hedge her bets, but Nick isn't cooperating."

"It's her own fault," Melanie said. "She kept after Jeffrey until the last minute."

"I think she's still after him now," said Cassie.

Jeffrey was just coming off the dance floor with Sally. His expression was the exact opposite of wintry; he looked as if he was having a wonderful time, flashing his lady-killing smile in all directions. Proud, Cassie thought, to have the Homecoming Queen on his arm. But it was funny, she thought the next minute, how quickly people stopped smiling when they ran into Faye.

Jeffrey tried to hustle Sally back onto the dance floor, but Faye moved as quickly as a stalking panther and cut them off. Then she and Sally stood on either side of Jeff, like a big, glossy black dog and a little rust-colored terrier fighting over a tall, slim bone.

"That's stupid," Laurel said. "Faye could have almost any guy here, but she only wants the ones who're a challenge."

"Well, it's not our problem," Melanie said sensibly. She turned to the outsider boy beside her and smiled, and they went together onto the dance floor. Laurel looked nettled for an instant, then smiled, shrugged at Cassie, and collected her own partner.

Cassie watched them go with a sinking heart. She'd been able to block out Adam's presence for the last few minutes, but here they were alone again. Determinedly, she looked around for some distraction. There was Jeffrey—he was in real trouble now. The music had started, Faye was smiling a lazy, dangerous smile at him, and Sally was bristling and looking daggers. The three of them were standing in a perfect triangle, nobody moving. Cassie didn't see how

95

Jeffrey was going to get out of it.

Then he looked up in her direction.

His reaction was startling. His eyes widened. He blinked. He stared at her as if he had never seen a girl before. Then he stepped away from Faye and Sally as if he'd forgotten their existence.

Cassie was dismayed, confused—but flattered. One thing—it certainly got her out of her present dilemma with Adam. When she turned and looked into Adam's eyes, she saw he understood, without even nodding.

Jeffrey was holding out his hand to her. She took it and let him lead her onto the dance floor. She cast one glance back at Adam and saw that his expression was a paradox: acceptance mixed with something darker, more disturbing.

It was another slow dance. Cassie held herself at a decent distance from Jeffrey, staring uncertainly down at his shoes. They were dark brown loafers with little tassels, the left one slightly scuffed. When she finally looked up at his face, her awkwardness vanished. That smile was not only blinding but openly admiring.

When we first met he was trying to impress me, Cassie thought dizzily. Now *he's* impressed.

She could see the appreciation in his eyes, feel it in the way he held her.

"We make a good couple," he said.

She laughed. Trust Jeffrey to compliment himself in complimenting her. "Thank you. I hope Sally isn't mad."

"It's not Sally I'm worried about. It's *her*."

"Faye. I know." She wished she had some advice for him. But nobody knew how to deal with Faye.

"Maybe you'd better be worried too. What's Diana going to say when she finds out you were here with Adam?"

"Diana *asked* me to come with him, because she was sick," Cassie said, flaring up in spite of herself. "I didn't even want to, and—"

"Hey. Hey. I was just teasing. Everybody knows Di and her prince consort are practically married. Although maybe she wouldn't have asked you if she'd known how beautiful you were going to look."

He was still teasing, but Cassie didn't like it. She looked around the dance floor and saw Laurel, who winked over her partner's shoulder. Suzan was dancing, too, very close with a muscular boy, her red-gold hair shining in the gloom.

And then it was over. Cassie looked up at Jeffrey and said, "Good luck with Faye," which was the best she could offer him. He flashed the smile again.

"I can handle it," he said confidently. "Don't you want to dance again? No? Are you sure?"

"Thanks, but I'd better get back," Cassie murmured, worried about the way he was looking at her. She managed to escape his restraining hand and started toward the sidelines, but before she could get there another boy asked her to dance.

She couldn't see Adam anywhere. Maybe he was off enjoying himself—she hoped so. She said "yes" to the boy.

It didn't stop with him. All sorts of guys, seniors and juniors, athletes and class officers, were coming up to her. She saw boys' eyes wander from their own dates to look at her as she danced.

I didn't know dances were like this. I didn't know *anything* was like this, she thought. For the moment she was entirely swept up in the magic of the night, and she pushed all troublesome reflection away. She let the music take her and let herself just be for a while.

Then she saw Sally's face on the sidelines.

Jeffrey wasn't with her. Cassie hadn't seen Jeffrey in a while. But Sally was focused on Cassie specifically, and her expression was venomous.

When that dance was over, Cassie evaded the next boy who tried to intercept her, and headed for Laurel. Laurel greeted her with glee.

"You're the belle of the ball," she said excitedly, tucking her arm through Cassie's and patting Cassie's hand. "Sally's furious. Faye's furious. *Everybody's* furious."

"It's the magnet perfume. I think Suzan used too much."

"Don't be silly. It's you. You're a perfect little—gazelle. No, a little white unicorn, one of a kind. I think even Adam has noticed."

Cassie went still. "Oh, I doubt that," she said lightly. "He's just being polite. You know Adam."

"Yes," said Laurel. "Sir Adam the Chivalrous. He turned around and asked Sally to dance after you left with Jeffrey, and Sally almost decked him."

Cassie smiled, but her heart was still pounding. She and Adam had promised not to betray their feelings for each other, not by word or look or deed—but they were making a horrible mess of things tonight on all fronts. Now she was afraid to look for Adam, and she didn't want to dance any more. She didn't want to be the belle of the ball; she didn't want every girl here to be furious with her. She wanted to go to Diana.

Suzan arrived, her extraordinary chest heaving slightly in her low-cut dress. She directed an arch smile at Cassie.

"I told you I knew what I was talking about," she said. "Having a good time?"

"Wonderful," Cassie said, digging her nails in one palm. She opened her mouth to say something else, but just then she glimpsed Sean making his way toward her. His face was eager, his usually slinking step purposeful.

"I should have warned you," Laurel said in an undertone. "Sean's been chasing you all night, but some other guy always got there first."

"If he *does* catch you he'll be all over you like ugly on an ape," Suzan added pleasantly, rummaging in her purse. "Oh, damn, I gave my lipstick to Deborah. Where *is* she?"

"Hi there," Sean said, reaching them. His small black eyes slid over Cassie. "So you're free at last."

"Not really," Cassie blurted. "I have to—go find Deborah for Suzan." What she had to do was get away from all this for a while. "I know where she is; I'll be right back," she continued to the startled Suzan and Laurel.

"I'll come along," Sean began instantly, and Laurel opened her mouth, but Cassie waved at both of them in dismissal.

"No, no—I'll go by myself. It won't take a minute," she said. And then she was away from them, plunging through the crowd toward the double doors.

She knew where the boiler room was, or at least where the door that led to it was. She'd never actually been inside. By the time she reached C-wing she'd left the music of the dance far behind.

The door marked CUSTODIAN'S OFFICE opened onto a long narrow room with unidentifiable machinery all around. Generators were humming, drowning out any other noise. It was cool and dank . . . spooky, Cassie thought. There were NO SMOKING signs on the walls and it smelled of oil and gas.

A stairway descended into the school basement. Cassie slowly went down the steps, gripping the smooth metal handrail. God, it's like going down into a tomb, she thought. Who would want to spend their time here instead of in the light and music up in the gym?

The boiler room itself smelled of machine oil and beer. It wasn't just cool; it was *cold*. And it was silent, except for the steady dripping of water somewhere.

A terrible place, Cassie thought shakily. All around her were machines with giant dials, and overhead there were huge pipes of all kinds. It was like being in the bowels of a ship. And it was deserted.

"Hello? Deborah?"

No answer.

"Debby? Chris? It's Cassie."

Maybe they couldn't hear her. There was another room behind the boiler room; she could glimpse it through an archway beyond the machines.

She edged toward it, worried about getting oil on Laurel's pristine dress. She looked through the archway and hesitated, gripped by a strange apprehension.

Drip. Drip.

"Is anybody there?"

A large machine was blocking her way. Uneasily, she poked her head around it.

At first she thought the room was empty, but then, at eye level, she saw something.

Something wrong. And in that instant her throat closed and her mind fragmented, single thoughts flashing across it like explosions from a flashbulb.

Swinging feet.

Swinging feet where feet shouldn't be. Somebody walking on air. Flying like a witch. Only, the feet weren't flying. They were swinging, back and forth, in two dark brown loafers. Two dark brown loafers with little tassels.

Cassie looked up at the face.

The relentless dripping of water went on. The smell of oil and stale alcohol nauseated her.

Can't scream. Can't do anything but gasp.

Drip and swing.

That face, that horrible blue face. No more lady-killer smile. I have to do something to help him, but how can I help? Nobody's neck bends that way when they're alive.

Every horrible detail was so clear. The fraying rope. The swinging shadow on the cinder-block wall. The machinery with its dials and switches. And the awful stillness.

Drip. Drip.

Swinging like a pendulum.

Hands covering her mouth, Cassie began to sob.

She backed away, trying not to see the curly brown hair on the head that was lolling sideways. He couldn't be dead when she'd just danced with him. He'd just had his arms around her, he'd flashed her that cocksure smile. And now—

She stepped back and hands fell on her shoulders.

She did try to scream then, but her throat was paralyzed. Her vision went dark.

"Steady. Steady. Hang on there."

It was Nick.

"Breathe slower. Put your head down."

"Nine-one-one," she gasped, and then, clearly and distinctly so that he would understand, "Call nine-one-one, Nick. Jeffrey—"

He cast a hard glance at the swinging feet. "He doesn't need a doctor. Do you?"

"I—" She was hanging on to his hand. "I came down to get Deborah."

"She's in the old science building. They got busted here."

"And I saw him—Jeffrey—"

Nick's arm was comforting, solid. "I get the picture," he said. "Do you want to sit down?"

"I can't. It's Laurel's dress." She was completely irrational, she realized. She tried desperately to get a grip on herself. "Nick, please let me go. I have to call an ambulance."

"Cassie." She couldn't remember him ever saying her name before, but now he was holding her shoulders and looking her directly in the face. "No ambulance is going to do him any good. You got that? Now just calm down."

Cassie stared into his polished-mahogany eyes, then slowly nodded. The gasping was easing up. She was grateful for his arm around her, although some part of her mind was standing back in disbelief—*Nick* was comforting her? Nick, who hated girls and was coldly polite to them at best?

"What's going on here?"

Cassie spun to see Adam in the archway. But when she tried to speak, her throat closed completely and hot tears flooded her eyes.

Nick said, "She's a little upset. She just found Jeffrey Lovejoy hanging from a pipe."

"*What?*" Adam moved swiftly to look around the machine. He came back looking grim and alert, his eyes glinting silver as they always did in times of trouble.

"How much do you know about this?" he asked Nick crisply.

"I came down to get something I left," Nick

said, equally short. "I found *her* about ready to keel over. And that's all."

Adam's expression had softened slightly. "Are you okay?" he said to Cassie. "I've been looking everywhere for you. I knew *something* was wrong, but I didn't know what. Then Suzan said you'd gone to look for Deborah, but that you were looking in the wrong place." As if it were the most natural thing in the world, he reached out to take her from Nick—and Nick resisted. For a moment there was tension between the two boys and Cassie looked from one to the other with dawning surprise and alarm.

She moved away from both. "I'm all right," she said. And, strangely, saying so made it almost true. It was partly necessity and partly something else—her witch senses were telling her something. She had a feeling of malice, of evil. Of darkness.

"The dark energy," she whispered.

Adam looked more keen and alert. "You think—?"

"*Yes,*" she said. "Yes, I do. But if only we could tell for sure . . ." Her mind was racing. Jeffrey. Jeffrey's body swinging like a pendulum. "*Usually we use clear quartz as a pendulum . . .*"

She snatched Melanie's necklace off and held it up, looking at the teardrop of quartz crystal.

"If the dark energy *was* here, maybe we can trace it," she said, fired with the idea. "See where it came from—or where it went. If you guys will help."

Nick was looking skeptical, but Adam cut in before he could speak. "Of course we'll help. But it's dangerous; we've got to be careful." His fingers gripped her arm reassuringly.

"Then—we have to go back in there," Cassie said, and before she could change her mind she moved, darting into the far room where the feet still swung. Nick and Adam were close behind her. Without letting herself think, she held the crystal up high, watching it shimmer in the light.

At first it just spun in circles. But then it began to seesaw violently, pointing out a direction.

O

SEVEN

Cassie followed the motion of the crystal. It was pointing upstairs, she decided—the opposite direction led into a wall.

"We'd better get out in the open, anyway," Adam said. "Otherwise we might not be able to follow it."

Cassie nodded. She and Adam were speaking quickly, tensely—but calmly. Their violent agitation was held just under the surface, kept down by sheer willpower. Having something to *do* was what made the difference, she thought as they climbed the stairs. She couldn't afford to have hysterics now; she had to keep her mind clear to trace Jeffrey's killer.

In the hallway outside the custodian's office

they ran into Deborah and the Henderson brothers.

"Adam, dude, what's goin' on?" Chris said. Cassie saw that he'd been drinking. "We were just comin' down for a little liquid refreshment, you know—"

"Not down there," Adam said shortly. He looked at Doug, who seemed less inebriated. "Go get Melanie," he said, "and tell her to call the police. Jeffrey Lovejoy's been murdered."

"Are you serious?" Deborah demanded. The fierce light was in her face again. "All right!"

"*Don't,*" said Cassie before she could stop herself. "You haven't seen him. It's terrible—and it's nothing to joke about."

Adam's arm shot out as Deborah started toward her. "Why don't you help us instead of picking fights with our side? We're trying to trace the dark energy that killed him."

"The dark energy," Deborah repeated scornfully.

Cassie took a quick breath, but Nick was speaking. "I think it's garbage too," he said calmly. "But if it *wasn't* the dark energy, that means a *person* did it—like somebody who had a grudge against Jeffrey." He stared at Deborah, his eyes hard.

Deborah stared back arrogantly. Cassie looked at her as she stood there in her short black tank dress—more like a sleeveless top than a dress—and her suede boots. Deborah was belligerent, antagonistic, hostile—and strong. For the first time in a long while Cassie noticed the crescent-moon tattoo on Deborah's collarbone.

"Why *don't* you help us, Deborah?" she said. "This crystal is picking something up—or it was before we all started talking. Help us find what it's tracing." And then she added, inspired by some instinct below the level of consciousness, "Of course, it's probably dangerous—"

"So what? You think I'm scared?" Deborah demanded. "All right, I'm coming. You guys get out of here," she told the Hendersons.

Somewhat to Cassie's surprise, Chris and Doug did, presumably going off to tell Melanie.

"All right," Cassie said, holding the crystal up again. She was afraid that it wouldn't do anything now that their concentration had been broken. And at first it simply hung at the end of the chain, swaying very slightly. But then, as the four of them stared at it, the swaying slowly became more pronounced. Cassie held her breath, trying to keep her hand from trembling. She didn't want to influence the crystal in any way.

It was definitely swinging now. In toward the boiler room and out toward the front of the school.

"Due east," Adam said in a low voice.

Holding the crystal high in her left hand, Cassie followed the direction of the swing, down the hallway.

Outside, the moon was almost full, high in the sky, dropping west behind them.

"The Blood Moon," Adam said quietly. Cassie remembered Diana saying that witches counted their year by moons, not months. The name of this one was hideously appropriate, but she didn't look back at it again. She was focusing on the crystal.

At first they walked through town, with closed stores and empty buildings on either side of them. Nothing stayed open past midnight in New Salem. Then the stores became less frequent, and there were a few clustered houses. Finally they were walking down a road which got lonelier and lonelier with every step, and all that surrounded them were the night noises.

There was no human habitation out here, but the moon was bright enough to see by. Their shadows stretched in front of them as they went. The air was cold, and Cassie shivered without taking her eyes off the crystal.

She felt something slip over her shoulders. Adam's jacket. She glanced at him gratefully, then quickly looked at the crystal again; if she faltered in her concentration it seemed to falter too, losing decisiveness and slowing almost to a random bobbing. It never swung as vigorously as the peridot had done for Diana—but then, Cassie *wasn't* Diana, and she didn't have a nearly-full coven to back her.

Behind her, she heard Adam say sharply, "Nick?" And then Deborah's derisive snort, "I wouldn't take it, anyway. I never get cold."

They were on a narrow dirt road now, still heading east. Suddenly Cassie had a terrible thought.

Oh, my God—*Faye's house*. That's where we set it loose and that's where we're going. We're going to trace this stuff all the way back to Faye's bedroom . . . and then what?

The coldness that went through her now was deeper and more numbing than the night wind. If the dark energy that had exploded through Faye's ceiling had killed Jeffrey, Cassie was as guilty as Faye was. She was a murderer.

Then stop tracing it, a thin voice inside her whispered. You're controlling the crystal; give it a twirl in the wrong direction.

But she didn't. She kept her eyes on the quartz teardrop, which seemed to shine with a milky light in the darkness, and she let it swing the way it wanted to.

If the truth comes out, it comes out, she told herself coldly. And if she was a murderer, she deserved to be caught. She was going to follow this trail wherever it led.

But it didn't seem to be leading to Crowhaven Road. They were still going east, not northeast. And suddenly the narrow, rutted road they were on began to seem familiar.

Up ahead she glimpsed a chain-link fence.

"The cemetery," Adam said softly.

"Wait," said Deborah. "Did you see—there, look!"

"At what, the cemetery?" Adam asked.

"No! At that thing—there it is again! Up there on the road."

"I don't see anything," Nick said.

"You have to. See, it's moving—"

"I see a shadow," Adam said. "Or maybe a possum or something . . ."

"No, it's big," Deborah insisted. "*There!* Can't you see that?"

Cassie looked up at last; she couldn't help it. The lonely road in front of her seemed dark and still at first, but then she saw—something. A shadow, she thought . . . but a shadow of what? It didn't lie along the road as a shadow ought to. It seemed to be standing high, and it was moving.

"I don't see anything," Nick said again, curtly.

"Then you're blind," Deborah snapped. "It's like a person."

Under Adam's jacket, Cassie's skin was rising in goose pimples. It *did* look like a person— except that it seemed to change every minute, now taller, now shorter, now wider, now thinner. At times it disappeared completely.

"It's heading for the cemetery," Deborah said.

"No—look! It's veering off toward the shed," Adam cried. "Nick, come on!"

Beside the road was an abandoned shed. Even in the moonlight it was clear that it was falling to pieces. The dim shape seemed to whisk toward it, merging with the darkness behind it.

Adam and Nick were running, Nick snarling,

"We're chasing after nothing!" Deborah was standing poised, tense and alert, scanning the roadside. Cassie looked at the chain in dismay. Everyone's concentration had been shattered, the crystal was gyrating aimlessly. She looked up to say something—and drew in a quick breath.

"There it is!"

It had reappeared beside the shed, and it was moving fast. It went *through* the chain-link fence.

Deborah was after it in an instant, running like a deer. And Cassie, without any idea of what she was doing, was right behind her.

"Adam!" she shouted. "Nick! This way!"

Deborah reached the waist-high fence and went over it, her tank dress not hindering her at all. Cassie reached it a second later, hesitated, then got a foothold in a chain link, flicking her skirts out of the way as she boosted herself over. She came down with a jolt that hurt her ankle, but there was no time to worry about it. Deborah was racing ahead.

"I've got it," Deborah shouted, suddenly pulling up short. "I've got it!"

Cassie could see it just in front of Deborah. It had stopped in its straight-line flight and was darting from side to side as if looking for escape. Deborah was darting, too, blocking it as if she were a guard on a basketball team.

We must be crazy, Cassie thought, as she reached the other girl. She couldn't leave Deborah to face the shadowy thing alone—but what were they going to do with it?

"Is there a spell or something to hold it?" she panted.

Deborah threw her a startled glance, and Cassie saw that she hadn't realized Cassie was behind her. "What?"

"We've got to trap it somehow! Is there a spell—"

"Down!" Deborah shouted.

Cassie dove for the ground. The shadow-thing had swelled suddenly to twice its size, like an infuriated cat, and then it had lunged at them. Straight at them. Cassie felt it rush over her head, colder than ice and blacker than the night sky.

And then it was gone.

Deborah and Cassie sat up and looked at each other.

Adam and Nick appeared, running. "Are you all right?" Adam demanded.

"Yes," Cassie said shakily.

"What were you two doing?" Nick said, looking at them in disbelief. And even Adam asked, "How did you get over the fence?"

Deborah gave him a scornful look. "I didn't mean *you*," he said.

Cassie gave him a scornful look. "Girls can climb," she said. She and Deborah stood up and began brushing each other off, exchanging a glance of complicity.

"It's gone now," Adam said, wisely dropping the subject of fences. "But at least we know what it looks like."

Nick made a derisive sound. "What *what* looks like?"

"You can't still say you didn't see it," Deborah said impatiently. "It was here. It went for Cassie and me."

"I saw something—but what makes you think it was this so-called dark energy?"

"We were tracing it," said Adam.

"How do we know what we were tracing?" Nick rapped back. "Something that was around the place Lovejoy was killed, that's all. It could be the 'dark energy'—or just some garden-variety ghost."

"A *ghost?*" Cassie said, startled.

"Sure. If you believe in them at all, some of

them like to hang out where murders are committed."

Deborah spoke up eagerly. "Yeah, like the Wailing Woman of Beverly, that lady in black that appears when somebody is going to die by violence."

"Or that phantom ship in Kennybunk—the *Isidore*. The one that comes and shows you your coffin if you're going to die at sea," Adam said, looking thoughtful.

Cassie was confused. She'd assumed it was the dark energy they were tracking—but who could tell? "It did end up in the cemetery," she said slowly. "Which seems like a logical place for a ghost. But if it wasn't the dark energy that killed Jeffrey, who was it? Who would *want* to kill him?"

Even as she asked, she knew the answer. Vividly, in her mind, she saw Jeffrey standing between two girls: one tall, dark, and disturbingly beautiful; the other small and wiry, with rusty hair and a pugnacious face.

"Faye or Sally," she whispered. "They were both jealous tonight. But—oh, look, even if they were mad enough to kill him, neither of them could have actually done it! Jeffrey was an athlete."

"A witch could have done it," Deborah said matter-of-factly. "Faye could've made him do it to himself."

"And Sally's got friends on the football team," Nick added dryly. "That's how she got herself voted Homecoming Queen. If they strangled him first, and then strung him up . . ."

Adam was looking disturbed at this cold-blooded discussion. "You don't actually believe that."

"Hey, a woman scorned, you know?" Nick said. "I'm not saying either of them did it. I'm saying either of them *could* have."

"Well, we won't figure it out by standing here," Cassie said, shivering. Adam's jacket had slipped off when she went over the fence. "Maybe if we could try to trace it again—"

It was then she realized she wasn't holding the crystal.

"It's gone," she said. "Melanie's crystal. I must have dropped it when that thing rushed us. It should be right here on the ground, then. It's *got* to be," she said.

But it wasn't. They all stooped to look, and Cassie combed through the sparse, withered grass with her fingers, but none of them could find it.

Somehow, this final disaster, incredibly tiny in comparison to everything that had happened that night, brought Cassie close to tears.

"It's been in Melanie's family for generations," she said, blinking hard.

"Melanie will understand," Adam told her gently. He put a hand on her shoulder, not easily but carefully, as if keenly aware that they were in front of witnesses.

"It's true, though; there's no point in standing around here," he said to the others. "Let's get back to school. Maybe they've found out something about Jeffrey there."

As Cassie walked, the Cinderella shoes hurting her feet and Laurel's silvery dress streaked with dirt, she found herself looking straight into the Blood Moon. It was hovering over New Salem like the Angel of Death, she thought.

Normally, on the night of the full moon, the Circle would meet and celebrate. But on the day after Jeffrey's murder Diana was still sick, Faye was refusing to speak to anyone, and no one else had the heart to call a meeting.

Cassie spent the day feeling wretched. Last night at the high school the police had found no leads as to Jeffrey's killer. They hadn't said if he'd been strangled first and then hung, or if he'd just been hung. They weren't saying much of anything, and they didn't like questions.

Melanie had been kind about the necklace, but Cassie still felt guilty. She'd used it to go off on what turned out to be a wild-goose chase, and then she'd lost it. But far worse was the feeling of guilt over Jeffrey.

If she hadn't danced with him, maybe Faye and Sally wouldn't have been so angry. If she hadn't let Faye have the skull, then the dark energy wouldn't have been released. However she looked at it, she felt responsible, and she hadn't slept all night for thinking about it.

"Do you want to talk?" her grandmother said, looking up from the table where she was cutting ginger root. The archaic kitchen which had seemed so bewildering to Cassie when she'd first come to New Salem was now a sort of haven. There was always something to do here, cutting or drying or preserving the herbs from her grandmother's garden, and there was often a fire in the hearth. It was a cheerful, homey place.

"Oh, Grandma," Cassie said, then stopped. She *wanted* to talk, yes, but how could she?

She stared at her grandmother's wrinkled hands spreading the root in a wooden rack for drying.

"You know, Cassie, that I'm always here for you—and so is your mother," her grandmother went on. She threw a sudden sharp glance up at the kitchen doorway, and Cassie saw that her mother was standing there.

Mrs. Blake's large dark eyes were fixed on Cassie, and Cassie thought there was something sad in them. Ever since they'd come on this "vacation" to Massachusetts, her mother had looked troubled, but these days there was a kind of tired wistfulness in her face that puzzled Cassie. Her mother was so beautiful, and so young-looking, and the new helplessness in her expression made her seem even younger than ever.

"And you know, Cassie, that if you're truly unhappy here—" her mother began, with a kind of defiance in her gaze.

Cassie's grandmother had stiffened, and her hands stopped spreading the root.

"—we don't have to stay," her mother finished.

Cassie was astounded. After all she'd been through those first weeks in New Salem, after all those nights she'd wanted to die from homesickness—*now* her mother said they could go? But even stranger was the way Cassie's grandmother was glaring.

"Running away has never solved anything," the older woman said. "Haven't you learned that yet? Haven't we all—"

"There are two children dead," Cassie's mother said. "And if Cassie wants to leave here, we will."

Cassie looked from one to the other in bewilderment. What were they talking about? "Mom," she said abruptly, "why did you bring me here?"

Her mother and grandmother were still looking at each other—a battle of wills, Cassie thought. Then Cassie's mother looked away.

"I'll see you at dinner," she said, and just as suddenly as she'd appeared, she slipped out of the room.

Cassie's grandmother let out a long sigh. Her old hands trembled slightly as she picked up another root.

"There are some things you can only understand later," she said to Cassie, after a moment. "You'll have to trust us for that, Cassie."

"Does this have something to do with why

you and Mom were estranged for so long? *Does it?*"

A pause. Then her grandmother said softly, "You'll just have to trust us . . ."

Cassie opened her mouth, then shut it again. There was no use in pressing it any further. As she'd already learned, her family was very good at keeping secrets.

She'd go to the cemetery, she decided. She could use the fresh air, and maybe if she found Melanie's crystal she would feel a little better.

Once there, she wished she'd asked Laurel to go along. Even though the October sun was bright, the air was nippy, and something about the dispirited graveyard made Cassie uneasy.

I wonder if ghosts come out in the daytime, she thought, as she located the place where she and Deborah had had to throw themselves facedown. But no ghosts appeared. Nothing moved except the tips of the grass which rippled in the breeze.

Cassie's eyes scanned the ground, looking for any glint of bright silver chain or clear quartz. She went over the area inch by inch. The chain *had* to be right here . . . but it wasn't. At last she gave up and sat back on her heels.

That was when she noticed the mound again.

She'd forgotten to ask her grandmother about it. She'd have to remember tonight. She got up and walked over to it, looking at it curiously.

By daylight, she could see that the iron door was rusty. The padlock was rusty too, but it looked fairly modern. The cement chunk in front of the door was large; she didn't see how it could have gotten there. It was certainly too heavy for a person to carry.

And why would somebody *want* to carry it there?

Cassie turned away from the mound. The graves on this side of the cemetery were modern too; she'd seen them before. The writing on the tombstones was actually legible. Eve Dulany, 1955–1976, she read. Dulany was Sean's last name; this must be his mother.

The next stone had two names: David Quincey, 1955–1976, and Melissa B. Quincey, 1955–1976. Laurel's parents, Cassie thought. God, it must be awful to have both your parents dead. But Laurel wasn't the only kid on Crowhaven Road who did. Right here beside the Quincey headstone was another marker: Nicholas Armstrong, 1951–1976; Sharon Armstrong, 1953–1976. Nick's mom and dad.

It must be.

When she saw the third headstone, the hairs on Cassie's arms began to prickle.

Linda Whittier, she read. Born 1954, died 1976. Suzan's mother.

Died 1976.

Sharply, Cassie turned to look at the Armstrong headstone again. She'd been right—both of Nick's parents had died in 1976. And the Quinceys . . . she was walking faster now. Yes. 1976 again. And Eve Dulany, too: died 1976.

Something rippled up Cassie's spine and she almost ran to the headstones on the far side of the mound. Mary Meade—Diana's mother— died 1976. Marshall Glaser and Sophia Burke Glaser. Melanie's parents. Died 1976. Grant Chamberlain. Faye's father. Died 1976. Adrian and Elizabeth Conant. Adam's parents. Died 1976.

Nineteen seventy-six. Nineteen seventy-six! There was a terrible shaking in Cassie's stomach and the hairs on the back of her neck were quivering.

What in God's name had happened in New Salem in 1976?

EIGHT

"It was a hurricane," Diana said.

It was Monday, and Diana was back in school, still a bit sniffly, but otherwise well. They were talking before American history class; it was the first chance Cassie had had to speak to Diana alone. She hadn't wanted to bring the question up in front of the others.

"A hurricane?" she said now.

Diana nodded. "We get them every so often. That year it hit with practically no warning, and the bridge to the mainland was flooded. A lot of people got caught on the island, and a lot of people got killed."

"I'm so sorry," Cassie said. Well, you see; there's a perfectly reasonable explanation after all, she was thinking. How could she have been so stupid as to have freaked out over this? A natural disaster explained everything. And when Cassie had asked her grandmother about the mound at the cemetery last night, the old woman had looked at her, blinking, and finally said, *was* there a mound at the old burying ground? If there was, it might be some sort of bunker—a place for storing ammunition in one of the old wars. Again, a simple explanation.

Laurel and Melanie came in and took seats in front of Cassie and Diana. Cassie took a deep breath.

"Melanie, I went back to the cemetery yesterday to look for your crystal—but I still couldn't find it. I'm sorry; I guess it's gone for good," she said.

Melanie's gray eyes were thoughtful and serious. "Cassie, I told you that night it didn't matter. The only thing I wish is that you and Adam and Nick and Deborah hadn't run off without the rest of us. It was dangerous."

"I know," Cassie said softly. "But right then it didn't *seem* dangerous—or at least, it did, but I didn't have time to think about how dangerous it really was. I just wanted to find whatever killed Jeffrey." She saw Melanie and Diana trade a glance; Melanie surprised and Diana rather smug.

Cassie felt vaguely uncomfortable. "Did Adam tell you anything about what we were talking about out in the cemetery?" she asked Diana. "About Faye and Sally?"

Diana sobered. "Yes. But it's all ridiculous, you know. Sally would never do anything like that, and as for Faye . . . well, she may be difficult at times, but she certainly isn't capable of killing anybody."

Cassie opened her mouth, and found herself looking at Melanie, whose gray eyes now reflected something like head-shaking cynicism. She looked back at Diana quickly and said, "No, I'm sure you're right," but she wasn't. Melanie was right; Diana was too trusting, too naive. Nobody knew better than Cassie just what Faye was capable of.

Ms. Lanning was starting class. Laurel and Melanie turned around, and Cassie opened her book and tried to keep her mind on history.

That entire school week was strange. Jeffrey's death had done something to the outsider students; it was different than the other deaths. Kori had been a Club member, or practically, and the principal hadn't been very popular. But Jeffrey was a football hero, one of their own, a guy just about everyone liked and admired. His death upset people in a different way.

The whispers started quietly. But by Wednesday Sally was saying openly that Faye and the Club had killed Jeffrey. Tension was building between Club members and the rest of the school. Only Diana seemed unaware of it, looking shocked when Melanie suggested that the Circle might not be welcome at Jeffrey's funeral. "We have to go," she said, and they did go, except Faye.

As for Faye . . . Faye spent the week quietly seething. She hadn't forgiven Suzan and Deborah for helping to get Cassie ready for the dance, she hadn't forgiven Nick for snubbing her, and she hadn't forgiven the rest of them for witnessing her humiliation. The only people she wasn't furious with were the Henderson brothers. When Jeffrey's death was mentioned, she looked hard and secretive.

Every day Cassie expected to get a phone call with some bizarre new demand, some new blackmail. But, for the moment, Faye seemed to be leaving her alone.

It was Friday afternoon, car-pooling home

after school, that Laurel mentioned the Halloween dance.

"Of course you're coming, Cassie," she said as they dropped Cassie off at Number Twelve. "You *have* to. And you've got plenty of time, two weeks, to think of somebody to ask."

Cassie walked into the house with her legs feeling weak. *Another* dance? She couldn't believe it.

One thing she knew: It couldn't be anything like the last one. She wouldn't let it be. She'd do what Laurel said, she'd find somebody to go with—and then she'd just stick with him the entire time. Somebody, anybody. Sean, maybe.

Cassie winced. Well, maybe not *anybody*. Starved for attention as he was, Sean might end up being a problem himself. She might never get rid of him.

No, Cassie needed some guy to be an escort and nothing else. Some guy who would absolutely not get interested in her, under any circumstances. Some guy who'd be completely indifferent . . .

A vision flashed through her mind, of mahogany eyes, rich and deep and absolutely dispassionate. Nick. Nick didn't even like girls. And Faye wouldn't care; Faye wasn't even speaking to Nick anymore. Nick would be safe—but would he ever want to go with her to a dance?

Only one way to find out, she thought.

Nick was Deborah's cousin, and lived with her parents at Number Two Crowhaven Road. The peach-colored house was run-down, and the garage was usually open, showing the car Nick was continually working on.

Adam had said it was a '69 Mustang coupe, which was something special. Right at the moment, though, it looked like a skeleton up on blocks.

When Cassie walked in late that afternoon, Nick was bent over the workbench, his dark hair shining faintly in the light of the naked bulb hanging from the rafters. He was doing something with a screwdriver to a part.

"Hi," Cassie said.

Nick straightened up. He didn't look surprised to see her, but then Nick never looked surprised. He didn't look particularly happy to see her either. He was wearing a T-shirt so covered with grease stains that it was difficult to read the slogan underneath, but faintly Cassie could make out the odd words *Friends don't let friends drive Chevys.*

Cassie cleared her throat. Just walk in and ask him, she'd thought—but now that was proving to be impossible. After a moment or two of staring at her, waiting, Nick looked back down at the workbench.

"I was just walking to Diana's," Cassie said brightly. "And I thought I'd stop by and say hi."

"Hi," Nick said, without looking up.

Cassie's mouth was dry. What had ever made her think she *could* ask a guy to a dance? So what if lots of guys had wanted to dance with her last time; that had probably just been a fluke. And *Nick* certainly hadn't been hanging around her.

She tried to make her voice sound casual. "So what are you doing . . ." She had meant to ask "for the Halloween dance" but her throat closed up and she panicked. Instead she finished in a squeak, " . . . right now?"

"Rebuilding the carburetor," Nick replied briefly.

"Oh," Cassie said. She searched her mind desperately for some other topic of conversation. "Um . . ." She picked up a little metal ball from the workbench. "So—what's this for?"

"The carburetor."

"Oh." Cassie looked at the little ball. "Uh, Nick, you know, I was just wondering"—she started to set the ball back down—"whether you might, um, want to—*oops*."

The ball had shot out of her sweaty fingers like a watermelon seed, landing with a *ping* somewhere under the workbench and disappearing. Cassie looked up, horrified, and Nick slammed down the screwdriver and swore.

"I'm sorry—honest, Nick, I'm sorry—"

"What the hell did you have to touch it for? What are you *doing* here, anyway?"

"I . . ." Cassie looked at his wrathful face and the last of her courage left her. "I'm sorry, Nick," she gasped again, and she fled.

Out of the garage and down the driveway. Without thinking she turned right when she got to the street, heading back for her own house. She didn't want to go to Diana's, anyway— Adam was probably there. She walked up Crowhaven Road, her cheeks still burning and her heart thumping.

It had been a stupid idea from the beginning. Suzan was right; Nick was an iguana. He didn't have any normal human emotions. Cassie hadn't expected him to *want* to go to the dance with her in the first place; she'd just thought maybe he wouldn't mind, because he'd been nice to her in the boiler room that night. But now he'd shown his true colors. She was just glad she hadn't actually asked him before she'd dropped the ball—that would have been the ultimate embarrassment.

Even as it was, though, her chest felt tight and hot and her eyes felt sore. She kept her head carefully high as she passed Melanie's house, and then Laurel's. She didn't want to see either of them.

The sun had just set and the color was draining out of everything. It gets dark so early these days, she was thinking, when the roar of a motor caught her attention.

It was a black Suzuki Samurai with the license plate FLIP ME. The Henderson brothers were in it, Doug driving too fast. As soon as they spotted her they pulled over and stuck their heads out the windows, shouting comments.

"Hey, what's a nice girl like you doing in a neighborhood like this?"

"You wanna party, Cassie?"

"C'mon, baby, we can show you a good time!"

They were just harassing her for the fun of it, but something made Cassie look up into Doug's

135

tilted blue-green eyes and say nervily, "Sure."

They stared at her, nonplussed. Then Chris burst into laughter.

"Cool; get in," he said, and opened the passenger side door.

"Wait a minute," Doug began, frowning, but Cassie was already getting in, Chris helping her up the high step. She didn't know what had possessed her. But she was feeling wild and irresponsible, which she guessed was the best way to be feeling when you were with the Henderson brothers.

"Where are we going?" she asked as they roared off. Chris and Doug looked at each other cagily.

"Gonna buy some pumpkins for Halloween," Chris said.

"Buy pumpkins?"

"Well, not *buy*, exactly," Chris temporized.

For some reason, at this particular moment, that struck Cassie as funny. She began to giggle. Chris grinned.

"We're goin' down to Salem," he explained. "They have the best pumpkin patches to raid. And if we get done early enough we can hide in the Witch Dungeon and scare the tourists."

The Witch Dungeon? thought Cassie, but all

she said was, "Okay."

The floor of the minijeep was littered with bottles, bits of pipe, rags, Dunkin' Donut bags, unraveling cassette tapes, and raunchy magazines. Chris was explaining to Cassie about how to construct a pipe bomb when they reached the pumpkin patch.

"Okay, now, shut up," Doug said. "We've gotta go around back." He turned the lights and engine off and cruised.

The pumpkin patch was a huge fenced enclosure full of pumpkins, some piled up, some scattered across the ground. Doug stopped the Samurai just behind a large pile by the booth where you paid for the pumpkins. It was fully dark now, and the light from the enclosure didn't quite reach them.

"Over the fence," Doug mouthed, and to Cassie: "Stay here." Cassie was glad he didn't want her to climb it; there was barbed wire at the top. Chris laid his jacket on it and the two boys swarmed over easily.

Then they calmly started handing pumpkins over the fence. Chris gave them to Doug, who stood on the pile and dropped them to Cassie on the other side, motioning her to put them in the back seat of the jeep.

What on earth do they *want* with all of these, anyway? Cassie wondered dizzily as she staggered back with armload after armload. Can you make a bomb out of a pumpkin?

"Okay," Doug hissed at last. "That's enough." He swarmed back over the fence. Chris started to climb over too, but just at that moment there was a frenzied barking and a large black dog with wiry legs appeared.

"Help!" squawked Chris. He was caught hanging over the top of the fence. The Doberman had him by the boot and was worrying it furiously, snarling. A man exploded out of the booth and began yelling at them and shaking his fist.

"Help! Help!" Chris shouted. He started to giggle and then yelped, "Ow! He's takin' my foot off! Ow! Help!"

Doug, his strange slanted eyes glittering wildly, rushed back to the jeep. "Gonna *kill* that dog," he said breathlessly. "Where's that army pistol?"

"Hold on, Max! Hold him till I get my shotgun!" the man was yelling.

"Ow! He's chewin' on me! It hurts, man!" Chris bellowed.

"Don't kill him," Cassie pleaded frantically,

catching Doug by the arm. All she needed was for him and the pumpkin man to start shooting at each other. Doug continued ransacking the litter on the jeep's floor. "Don't kill the dog! We can just give him this," Cassie said, suddenly inspired. She snatched up a Dunkin' Donuts bag with several stale doughnuts in it. While Doug was still looking for a gun, she ran back to the fence.

"Here, doggy, nice doggy," she gasped. The dog snarled. Chris continued bellowing; the pumpkin man continued yelling. "*Good* dog," Cassie told the Doberman desperately. "Good boy, here, look, doughnuts, see? Want a doughnut?" And then, surprising herself completely, she shouted, "*Come here! NOW!*"

At the same time, she did—she didn't know what. She did . . . something . . . with her mind. She could feel it going out of her like a blast of heat. It hit the dog and the dog let go of Chris's foot, hind legs collapsing. Belly almost on the ground, it slunk over to the fence and crouched.

Cassie felt tall and terrible. She said, "Good dog," and tossed the doughnut bag over the fence. Chris was scrambling over in the other direction, almost falling on his head. The dog lay down and whined pitifully, ignoring the doughnuts.

"Let's go," Chris yelled. "Come on, Doug! We don't need to kill anybody!"

Between them, he and Cassie bundled the protesting Doug into the jeep and Chris drove off. The pumpkin-seller ran after them with his shotgun, but when they reached the road he gave up the chase.

"Ow," Chris said, shaking his foot and causing the jeep to veer.

Doug muttered to himself.

Cassie leaned back and sighed.

"Okay," Chris said cheerfully, "now let's go to the Witch Dungeon."

The Salem Witch Dungeon Museum looked like a house from the outside. Chris and Doug seemed to know the layout well, and Cassie followed them around the house, where they slipped in a back entrance.

Through a doorway Cassie glimpsed what seemed to be a small theater. "That's where they do the witch trials," Chris said. "You know, like a play for the tourists. Then they take 'em down here."

A flight of narrow stairs plunged down

into darkness.

"*Why?*" Cassie said.

"It's the dungeon. They give 'em a tour. We hide in the corners and jump up and yell when they get close. Some of 'em practically have heart attacks," Doug said, with his mad grin.

Cassie could see how that might happen. As they made their way down the stairs it got darker and darker. A dank, musty odor assaulted her nostrils and the air felt very cool.

A narrow corridor stretched forward into the blackness, which was broken only by tiny lights at long intervals. Small cells opened out from either side of the corridor. The whole place had a heavy, underground feel to it.

It's like the boiler room, Cassie thought. Her feet stopped moving.

"Come on, what's wrong?" Doug whispered, turning around. She could barely see him.

Chris came back to the foot of the stairs and looked into her face. "We don't have to go in there yet," he said. "We can wait here till they start to come down."

Cassie nodded at him gratefully. It was bad enough standing on the edge of this terrible place. She didn't want to go in until she absolutely had to.

"Or . . ." Chris seemed to be engaging in some prodigious feat of thought. "Or . . . we could just *leave*, you know."

"Leave now? Why?" Doug demanded, running back.

"Because . . ." Chris stared at him. "Because . . . because I say so!"

"You? Who cares what you say?" Doug returned in a whispering shout and the two of them began to scuffle.

They're not really scary after all, Cassie thought, a little dazedly. They're more like the Lost Boys in *Peter Pan*. Peculiar, but sort of cute.

"It's all right," she said, to stop their fighting. "We can stay. I'll just sit down on the stairs."

Out of breath, they sat down too, Chris massaging the toe of his boot.

Cassie leaned against the wall and shut her eyes. She could hear voices from above, someone talking about the Salem witch trials, but only snatches of the lecture got through to her. She was drained from everything that had happened today, and this dreadful place made her feel sick and fuzzy. As if she had cobwebs in her brain.

A woman's voice was saying, ". . . the royal

governor, Sir William Phips, established a special court to deal with the cases. By now there were so many accused witches . . ."

So many fake witches, Cassie thought hazily, half listening. If that woman only knew about the real witches lurking in her dungeon.

". . . on June tenth, the first of the convicted witches was publicly executed. Bridget Bishop was hung on Gallows Hill, just outside of Salem . . ."

Poor Bridget Bishop, Cassie thought. She had a sudden vision of Jeffrey's swinging feet and a wave of nausea passed over her. Probably Bridget's feet had been swinging when they hung her, too.

". . . by the end of September eighteen other people had been hung. Sarah Goode's last words . . ."

Eighteen. That's a lot of swinging feet. God, I don't feel well, thought Cassie.

". . . and a nineteenth victim was pressed to death. Pressing was a form of Puritan torture in which a board was placed on the victim's chest, and then heavier and heavier rocks were piled on top of the board . . ."

Ugh. Now I *really* don't feel well. Wonder how it feels to have rocks piled on you till you die? Guess I'll never know since that doesn't happen much today. Unless you happen to be caught in a rockslide, or something . . .

With a jerk, Cassie sat up straight, the cobwebs swept out of her brain as if by a blast of icy wind.

Rockslide. Avalanche. Mr. Fogle, the high-school principal, had found out what it was like to have rocks piled on you till you died.

Weird coincidence. That was all it was. But . . .

Oh, my God, Cassie thought suddenly.

She felt as if her entire body were plugged into something electric. Her thoughts were tumbling over each other.

Rockslide. Pressed to death. Same thing, really. And hanging. The witches were hanged . . . just like Jeffrey Lovejoy. Oh, God, oh, God. There had to be a connection.

". . . never know how many died in prison. In comparison to the conditions there, the swift oblivion of a broken neck may have been merciful. Our tour will now take you—"

Broken neck. A broken neck.

Kori's neck had been broken.

Cassie thought she was going to faint.

NINE

The voices from above were getting nearer. Cassie couldn't move; a gray blanket seemed to have enfolded her senses. Chris was pulling at her arm.

"C'mon, Cassie! They're comin'!"

Faintly, Cassie heard from above: "If you'll line up in single file, we'll be going down a narrow stairway . . ."

Chris was pulling Cassie off the narrow stairway. "Hey, Doug, give me a hand here!"

Cassie made a supreme effort. "We have to go home," she said urgently to Chris. She drew herself up and tried to speak with authority. "I have to go back and tell Diana—something—right now."

The brothers looked at each other, perplexed but dimly impressed.

"Okay," Chris said, and Cassie sagged, the grayness washing over her again.

With Doug pulling in front and Chris trying to prop her up from behind, they led her rapidly through the dark, winding corridors of the dungeon. They seemed as comfortable in the darkness as rats, and they guided her unerringly through the passageways until a neon sign announced EXIT.

On the drive north, the pumpkins thumped and rolled in the back seat like a load of severed heads. Cassie kept her eyes shut and tried to breathe normally. The one thing she knew was that she couldn't tell the Henderson brothers what she was thinking. If they found out what she suspected about Kori, anything might happen.

"Just drop me off at Diana's," she said when they finally returned to Crowhaven Road. "No—you don't have to go in with me. Thanks."

"Okay," Chris said, and they let her off. Then he stuck his head back out the window. "Uh, hey—thanks for getting that mutt off me," he said.

"Sure," Cassie said light-headedly. "Any time." As they rolled away she realized they had never even asked her why she needed to talk to Diana. Maybe they were so used to doing inexplicable things themselves that they didn't wonder when other people did.

Mr. Meade answered the door, and Cassie realized that it must be late if he was home from the office. He called up to Diana as Cassie climbed the stairs.

"Cassie!" Diana said, jumping up as she saw Cassie's face. "What's the matter?"

Adam was sitting on the bed; he rose too, looking alarmed.

"I know it's late—I'm sorry—but we have to talk. I was in the Witch Dungeon—"

"You were where? Here, take this; your hands are like ice. Now start over again, slowly," Diana said, sitting her down and wrapping her in a sweater.

Slowly, stumbling sometimes, Cassie told them the story: how Chris and Doug had picked her up and taken her to Salem. She left out the part about the pumpkin patch, but told how they'd gone to the Witch Dungeon, and how, listening to the lecture, she had suddenly seen the connection. Pressing to death—

147

rockslides; hanging—broken necks.

"But what does it mean?" Diana said when she'd finished.

"I don't know, exactly," Cassie admitted. "But it looks like there's some connection between the three deaths and the way Puritans used to punish people."

"The dark energy is the connection," Adam said quietly. "That skull was used by the original coven, which lived in the time of the witch trials."

"But that wouldn't account for Kori," Diana protested. "We didn't activate the skull until after Kori was dead."

Adam was pale. "No. But I found the skull the day before Kori died. I took it out of the sand . . ." His eyes met Cassie's, and she had a terrible feeling of dismay.

"Sand. 'To Hold Evil Harmless,'" she whispered. She looked at Diana. "That's in your Book of Shadows. Burying an object in sand or earth to hold the evil in it harmless. Just like—" She stopped abruptly and bit her tongue. God, she'd almost said, "Just like you buried the skull on the beach to keep it safe."

"Just like I found it," Adam finished for her. "Yes. And you think that when I took it out, that alone activated it. But that would mean the skull would have to be so strong, so powerful . . ." His voice trailed off. Cassie could see he was trying to fight the idea; he didn't want to believe it. "I did feel *something* when I pulled it out of that hole," he added quietly. "I felt dizzy, strange. That could have been from dark energy escaping." He looked at Cassie. "So you think that energy came to New Salem and killed Kori."

"I—don't know what to think," Cassie said wretchedly. "I don't know why it *would*. But it can't be coincidence that every single time we interact with the skull, somebody dies afterward, in a way that the Puritans used to kill witches."

"But don't you see," Diana said excitedly, "it *isn't* every time. Nobody used the skull right before Jeffrey died. It was absolutely safe—" She hesitated and then went on quickly. "Well, of course I can tell *you* two—it was safe out on the beach. It's still buried there now. I've been checking it every few days. So there isn't a one-to-one correspondence."

Cassie was speechless. Her first impulse was to blurt out, "Somebody did too use the skull!" But that would be insane. She could never tell

Diana that—and now she was utterly at a loss. A shaking was starting deep inside her. Oh, God, there was a one-to-one correspondence.

It was like that slogan, *Use a gun; go to jail.* Use the skull; kill somebody. And she, Cassie, was responsible for the last time the skull had been used. She was responsible for killing Jeffrey.

Then she got another terrible jolt. She found Adam's keen blue-gray eyes fixed on her. "I know what you're thinking," he said.

Cassie swallowed, frozen.

"You're trying to think of a way to protect me," he said. "Neither of you likes the idea that my pulling the skull out of the sand had something to do with Kori's death. So you're trying to discredit the theory. But it won't work. There's obviously *some* connection between the skull and all three deaths—even Kori's."

Cassie still couldn't move. Diana touched his hand.

"If it is true," she said, her green eyes blazing with intensity, "then it isn't your fault. You couldn't know that removing the skull would do any harm. You couldn't *know.*"

But I did know, Cassie thought. Or at least I

should have known. I knew the skull was evil; I sensed it was capable of killing. And I still let Faye take it. I should have fought her harder; I should have done anything to stop her.

"If anyone's to blame," Diana was going on, "it's me. I'm the coven leader; it was my decision to use the skull in the ceremony. If the dark energy that knocked Faye over went out and killed Mr. Fogle and Jeffrey afterward, it's my fault."

"No, it isn't," Cassie said. She couldn't stand any more. "It's mine—or at least it's everybody's . . ."

Adam looked from one girl to the other, then burst into strained laughter and dropped his head into his hand.

"Look at us," he said. "Trying to clear each other and each take the blame ourselves. What a joke."

"Pretty pathetic," Diana agreed, trying to smile.

Cassie was fighting tears.

"I think we'd better stop thinking about whose fault it is, and start thinking about what to do," Adam went on. "If the dark energy that escaped at the ceremony killed both Mr. Fogle and Jeffrey, it may still be out there. It may do something else. We need to think about ways to stop it."

They talked for several hours after that. Adam thought they should search for the dark energy, maybe do some scrying around the graveyard. Diana thought they should continue combing all the Books of Shadows, even the most indecipherable ones, to see if there was any advice about dealing with evil like this, and to learn more about the skull.

"And about Black John, too," Cassie suggested mechanically, and Diana and Adam agreed. Black John had used the skull in the beginning, had "programmed" it. Perhaps his intentions were still affecting it.

But all the time they were talking, Cassie was feeling—outside. Alienated. Adam and Diana really *were* good, she thought, watching them talk fervently, fired with the discussion. They really had acted with the best of intentions. She, Cassie, was different. She was—evil.

Cassie knew things that they didn't know. Things she could never tell them.

Diana was nice when the time came for Cassie to go. "Adam had better drive you home," she said.

Adam did. They didn't speak until they

reached Cassie's house.

"How're you hanging on?" he said quietly then.

Cassie couldn't look at him. She had never wanted comfort more, never wanted to throw herself into his arms as much as she did now. She wanted to tell him the whole story about Faye and the skull, and listen to him say that it was all right, that she didn't have to face it alone. She wanted him to hold her.

She could feel him wanting that too, just inches away in the driver's seat.

"I'd better go inside," she said shakily.

Adam was gripping the steering wheel so hard it looked as if he were trying to break it.

"Good night," she said softly, still without looking at him.

There was a long, long pause while she felt Adam fight with himself. Then he said, "Good night, Cassie," in a voice drained of all energy.

Cassie went inside. She couldn't talk to her mother or her grandmother about this either, of course. She could just imagine it: "Hi, Mom; you remember Jeffrey Lovejoy? Well, I helped kill him." No, thank you.

It was a strange thought, knowing you were evil. It floated around in Cassie's mind as she lay in bed that night, and just before she fell asleep it got weirdly mixed up with visions of Faye's honey-colored eyes.

Wicked, she could almost hear Faye chuckling throatily. You're not evil, you're just *wicked* . . . like me.

The dream started out beautifully. She was in her grandmother's garden, in the summer, when everything was blossoming. Lemon balm spilled a golden pool on the ground. Lavender, lily of the valley, and jasmine were throwing such sweet scents into the air that Cassie felt giddy.

Cassie bent to snap off a stem of honeysuckle, with its tiny, creamy flowerheads. The sun shone down, warming her shoulders. The sky was clear and spacious. Strangely, although this was her grandmother's garden, there was no house nearby. She was all alone in the bright sunshine.

Then she saw the roses.

They were huge, velvety, red as rubies. No roses like that grew wild. Cassie took a step toward them, then another. Dew stood in the curl of one of the rose petals, quivering slightly. Cassie wanted to smell one of them, but she was afraid.

She heard a throaty chuckle beside her.

"Faye!"

Faye smiled slowly. "Go ahead, smell them," she said. "They won't bite you." But Cassie shook her head. Her heart was beating quickly.

"Oh, come on, Cassie." Faye's voice was coaxing now. "Look over there. Doesn't that look interesting?"

Cassie looked. Behind the roses something impossible had happened. Night had fallen, even though it was still daylight where Cassie was standing. It was a cool black-and-purple night, broken by stars but not a trace of moon.

"Come with me, Cassie," Faye coaxed again. "It's just a few little steps. I'll show you how easy it is." She walked behind the rosebush and Cassie stared at her. Faye was standing in darkness now, her face shadowed, her glorious hair merging with the gloom.

"You might as well," Faye told her softly, inexorably. "After all, you're already like me— or had you forgotten? You've already made your choice."

Cassie's hand let the honeysuckle spray fall. Slowly, slowly, she reached out and picked one of the roses. It was such a deep red, and so soft.

Cassie stared down into it.

"Beautiful, isn't it?" Faye murmured. "Now bring it here."

Mesmerized, Cassie took a step. There was a line of wavering shadow on the ground, between the darkness and the day. Cassie took another step and a sudden sharp pain in her finger made her gasp.

The rose had pricked her. Blood was streaming down her wrist. All the thorns on the roses were crimson, as if they'd been dipped in blood.

Appalled, she looked up at Faye, but she saw only darkness and heard only that mocking chuckle. "Maybe next time," Faye's voice floated out of the shadows.

Cassie woke up with her heart pounding, eyes staring into the blackness of her room. When she turned the light on, she almost expected to see blood on her arm. But there was no blood, and no mark of any thorn on her finger.

Thank God, she thought. It was a dream, just a dream. Still, it was a long time before she could fall asleep again.

She woke again to the ringing of the phone.

By the color of the light against the eastern window she knew she'd slept late.

"Hello?"

"Hello, Cassie," a familiar voice said in her ear.

Cassie's heart jumped. Instantly the entire dream flashed before her. In a panic, she expected Faye to start talking throatily about roses and darkness.

But Faye's voice was ordinary. "It's Saturday, Cassie. Do you have any plans for tonight?"

"Uh . . . no. But—"

"Because Deborah and Suzan and I are having a little get-together. We thought you might like to come."

"Faye . . . I thought you were mad at me."

Faye laughed. "I was a little—miffed, yes. But that's over now. I'm *proud* of your success with the guys. It just shows you what a little witchery will do, hmm?"

Cassie ignored this; she'd had a sudden thought. "Faye, if you're planning to use the skull again, forget it. Do you want to know how dangerous it is?" She started to tell Faye what she'd discovered in the Witch Dungeon, but Faye interrupted.

"Oh, who cares about the skull anymore?"

she said. "This is a *party*. So we'll see you at around eight, then, all right? You *will* show up, won't you, Cassie? Because there might be— unfortunate consequences if you didn't. 'Bye!"

Deborah and Suzan will be there, Cassie told herself as she walked up to Faye's house that night. They won't let Faye actually kill me. The thought gave her some comfort.

And Faye, when she opened the door, seemed less sinister than usual. Her golden eyes were glimmering with something like mischief and her smile was almost playful.

"Come in, Cassie. Everybody's in the den," she said.

Cassie could hear music as they approached a room off the entrance hall. It was furnished in the same opulent and luxurious style as the rest of the house. Noise from a huge TV was competing with some song by Madonna being blasted out of a magnificent stereo unit. With all this technology, the dozens of candles stuck in various kinds of holders around the room seemed incongruous.

"Turn that stuff down," Faye ordered. Suzan, pouting, pointed a remote control at the stereo, while Deborah muted the TV. Apparently Faye had forgiven them as well.

"Now," Faye said, with a feline smile at Cassie, "I'll explain. The housekeeper has the day off, and my mother is sick in bed—"

"As usual," Deborah interrupted, to Cassie. "Her mom spends ninety-five percent of her life in bed. Nerves."

Faye's eyebrows arched and she said, "Yes, well, it's certainly *convenient*, isn't it? At times like this." She turned back to Cassie and went on, "So we're going to have a little pizza party. You'll help out getting things ready, won't you?"

Cassie was tingling with relief. A pizza party. She'd been imagining—oh, all sorts of strange things. "I'll help," she said.

"Then let's get started. Suzan will show you what to do."

Cassie followed Suzan's directions. They lit the red and pink candles and started a low, crackling fire in the fireplace. They lit incense, too, which Suzan said was composed of ginger root, cardamom, and neroli oil. It was pungent, but delicious smelling.

Faye, meanwhile, was placing crystals about the room. Cassie recognized them—garnets and carnelians, fire opals and pink tourmelines. And Suzan, Cassie noticed, was wearing a carnelian necklace which harmonized with her strawberry-blond hair, while Faye was wearing more than her usual number of star rubies.

Deborah switched off the lamps and went to fiddle with the stereo. The music that began to rise was like nothing Cassie had ever heard. It was low and throbbing, some primal beat that seemed to get into her blood. It started out softly, but seemed to be getting almost imperceptibly louder.

"All right," Faye said, standing back to survey their work. "It's looking good. I'll get the drinks."

Cassie looked over the room herself. Warm; it looked warm and inviting, especially when compared with the chilly October weather outside. The candles and the fire made a rosy glow, and the soft, insistent music filled the air. The incense was spicy, intoxicating, and somehow sensuous, and the smoke threw a slight haze over the room.

It looks like an opium den or something, Cassie thought, simultaneously fascinated and horrified, just as Faye came back with a silver tray.

Cassie stared. She'd expected, maybe, a six-pack of soda—or maybe a six-pack of something else, knowing Deborah. She should have known Faye would never stoop to anything so inelegant. On the tray was a crystal decanter and eight small crystal glasses. The decanter was half full of some clear ruby-colored liquid.

"Sit down," Faye said, pouring into four of the glasses. And then, at Cassie's doubtful look, she smiled. "It's not alcoholic. Try it and see. Oh, go *on*."

Warily, Cassie took a sip. It had a subtle, faintly sweet taste and it made her feel flushed with warmth right down to her fingertips.

"What's in it?" she asked, peering into her glass.

"Oh, this and that. It's—stimulating, isn't it?"

"Mmm." Cassie took another sip.

"And now," Faye smiled, "we can play Pizza Man."

There was a pause, then Cassie said, "Pizza Man?"

"Pizza Man He Delivers," Suzan said, and giggled.

"Otherwise known as watching guys make fools of themselves," Deborah said, grinning savagely. She might have gone on, but Faye interrupted.

"Let's not *tell* Cassie; let's just show her," she

said. "Where's the phone?" Deborah handed her a cordless phone.

Suzan produced the yellow pages, and after a few moments of thumbing and scanning, read out a number.

Faye dialed. "Hello?" she said pleasantly. "I'd like to order a large pizza, with pepperoni, olives, and mushrooms." She gave her address and phone number. "That's right, New Salem," she said. "Can you tell me how long it will be? All right; thanks. 'Bye."

She hung up, looked at Suzan, and said, "Next."

And then, to Cassie's growing astonishment, she did it all over again.

Six times.

By the end of it, Faye had ordered seven large pizzas, all with the same toppings. Cassie, who was feeling somewhat dizzy from the smell of incense, wondered just how many people Faye was planning to feed.

"Who's coming to this party—the entire Mormon Tabernacle Choir?" she whispered to Suzan. Suzan dimpled.

"I hope not. It's not choirboys we're interested in."

"That's enough," said Faye. "Just wait, Cassie,

and you'll see."

When the doorbell rang the first time, Faye, Suzan, and Deborah went into the parlor and looked through the window. Cassie followed and looked too. The porch light revealed a young man holding a greasy cardboard box.

"Hmm," said Faye. "Not bad. Not terrific, but not bad."

"I think he's fine," Suzan said. "Look at those shoulders. Let's take him."

With Cassie trailing behind, they all went into the hall.

"Well, hello," Faye said, opening the door. "Do you mind coming inside and putting it over here? I left my purse in the other room." As Cassie watched with widening eyes, they escorted the guy into the warmth of the luxurious, richly scented den. Cassie saw him blink, then saw a stupefied expression cross his face.

Deborah took the pizza from him. "You know," Faye said, biting the pen she had poised over a checkbook, "you look a little tired. Why don't you sit down? Are you thirsty?"

Suzan was pouring a glassful of the clear ruby liquid. She held it out to him with a smile. The delivery boy wet his lips, looking dazed.

Cassie could understand why. She thought there was probably no guy in the world who could resist Suzan, with her cloud of strawberry-gold hair and her low-cut blouse, holding out a crystal glass. Suzan leaned over a little farther as she offered it to him, and the guy took the drink.

Deborah and Faye exchanged knowing glances. "I'll go move his car around the side," Deborah murmured, and left.

"My name's Suzan," Suzan said to the guy, as she sank into the cushiony couch beside him. "What's yours?"

Deborah had barely returned when the doorbell rang again.

TEN

"Yuck," Deborah said, as they peered out the parlor window again. This delivery guy was skinny, with lank hair and acne.

Faye was already moving to the front door. "Pizza? We didn't order any pizza. I don't care who you called to confirm it, we don't want it." She shut the door in his face, and after a few minutes of hanging around the porch he went away.

As his delivery van was pulling out, another one pulled in. The tall, blond guy with the cardboard box kept looking behind him at the receding rival van as he walked to the door.

"Now *this* is more like it," Faye said.

When they brought the blond delivery guy

into the den, Suzan and the muscular one were entangled on the couch. The pair disengaged themselves, the boy still looking foggy, and Faye poured the new guest a drink.

Within the next hour, the doorbell rang four more times and they collected two more delivery boys. Suzan divided her attention between the muscular one and a new one with high cheekbones who said he was part Native American. The other new one, who looked younger than the others and had soft-brown eyes, sat nervously next to Cassie.

"This is weird," he said, looking around the room, and taking another gulp from his glass. "This is so weird . . . I don't know what I'm doing. I've got deliveries to make . . ." Then he said, "Gee, you're pretty."

Gee? thought Cassie. Gosh. Golly. Oh, my *God.* "Thanks," she said weakly, and glanced around the room for help.

None was forthcoming. Faye, looking sultry and exuding sensuality, was running one long crimson fingernail up and down the blond guy's sleeve. Suzan was sunk deep in the couch with an admirer on either side. Deborah was sitting on the arm of an overstuffed chair, eyes slitted and rather scornful.

"Can I put my arm around you?" the brown-eyed boy was asking hesitantly.

Boys aren't toys, Cassie thought. Even if this one did look like a teddy bear. Faye had brought these guys here to play with, and that was wrong . . . wasn't it? They didn't know what they were doing; they didn't have any *choice.*

"I just moved up here last summer from South Carolina," the boy was going on. "I had a girl back there . . . but now I'm so lonely . . ."

Cassie knew the feeling. This was a *nice* guy, her age, and his brown eyes, though a little glassy, were appealing. She didn't scream when he put his arm around her, where it rested warmly and a little awkwardly around her shoulders.

She felt light-headed. Something about the incense . . . or the crystals, she thought. The music seemed to be pulsing inside her. She should be embarrassed by what was going on in this room—she *was* embarrassed—but there was something exciting about it too.

Some of the candles had gone out, making it darker.

The warmth around Cassie's shoulders was nice. She thought of yesterday night, when

167

she'd wanted so much for someone to comfort her, to hold her. To make her feel not alone.

"I don't know why, but I really like you," the brown-eyed boy was saying. "I never felt like this before."

Why not do it? She was already—bad. And she wanted to be close to *somebody*. . . .

The brown-eyed boy leaned in to kiss her.

That was when Cassie knew it was wrong. Not the way kissing Adam was wrong, but wrong for *her*. She didn't want to kiss him. Every individual cell in her body was protesting, panicking. She wiggled out from under him like an eel and jumped up.

Faye and the blond guy were also on their feet, heading out of the room. So were Suzan and her unmatched pair.

"We're just going upstairs," Faye said in her husky voice. "There's more room up there. Lots of rooms, in fact."

"No," Cassie said.

A hint of a frown creased Faye's forehead, then she smiled and went over to Cassie, speaking in low tones. "Cassie, I'm disappointed in you," she said. "After your performance at the dance, I really thought you were one of us. And it's not *nearly* as wicked as some other things you've done. You can do anything you want with these guys, and they'll like it."

"No," Cassie said again. "You told me to come over and I did. But I don't want to stay." Her eyes were smarting and she had trouble keeping her voice steady.

Faye looked exasperated. "Oh, all right. If you don't want to have fun, I can't make you. Go."

Relief washed over Cassie. With one glance back at the brown-eyed boy, she hurried to the door. After last night's dream, she'd been so frightened . . . she hadn't been sure what Faye would do to her. But she was getting away.

Faye's voice caught her at the door, and she waited until she had Cassie's full attention before speaking.

"Maybe next time," she said.

Cassie's entire skin was tingling as she hurried away from Faye's house. She just wanted to get home, to be safe. . . .

"Hey, wait a minute," Deborah called after her.

Reluctantly, Cassie turned and waited. She was braced as if for a blow.

Deborah came up quickly, her step light and controlled as always. Her dark hair was tumbling in waves around her small face and falling into her eyes. Her chin was slightly outthrust as usual, but her expression wasn't hostile.

"I'm leaving too. You want a ride?" she said.

Instantly memories of the last "ride" she'd accepted flashed through Cassie's mind. But she didn't exactly like to refuse Deborah. After Faye's parting words, Cassie was feeling small and soft and vulnerable—like something that could be easily squashed. And besides . . . well, it wasn't often Deborah made a gesture like this.

"Okay, thanks," Cassie said after only a moment's hesitation. She didn't ask if they should be wearing helmets. She didn't think Deborah would appreciate the question.

Cassie had never been on a motorcycle before. It seemed bigger when she was trying to get on it than it had looked just standing there. Once she was on, though, it felt surprisingly stable. She wasn't afraid of falling off.

"Hang on to me," Deborah said. And then, with an incredibly loud noise, they were moving.

It was the most exhilarating feeling—flying through the air. Like witches on broomsticks, Cassie thought. Wind roared in Cassie's face, whipped her hair back. It whipped Deborah's hair into Cassie's eyes so she couldn't see.

As Deborah accelerated, it became terrifying. Cassie was sure she'd never gone this fast before. The wind felt icy cold. They were racing forward into darkness, far too fast for safety on a rural road. The houses on Crowhaven were far behind. Cassie couldn't breathe, couldn't speak. Everything was the wind and the road and the feeling of speed.

I'm going to die, Cassie thought. She almost didn't care. Something this electrifying was worth dying for. She was sure Deborah couldn't take this next corner.

"Relax!" Deborah shouted, her voice snatched away by the wind. "Relax! Don't fight the way I'm leaning."

How can you relax when you're plunging at practically a hundred miles an hour into darkness? Cassie thought. But then she found out how: you give yourself up to it. Cassie resigned herself to her fate, and let the speed and the wind take her. And, magically, everything was all right.

She was aware, eventually, that they were heading back up Crowhaven Road, past Diana's house, past the others. They overshot Cassie's house and stormed around the vacant lot at the point of the headland.

Dust sprayed up on either side. Cassie saw the cliff whip by and buried her head in Deborah's shoulder. Then they were leaning, they were slowing, they were spiraling to a stop.

"So," said Deborah, when the world was still again, "what'd you think?"

Cassie lifted her head and made her fingers stop clutching. Every inch of her was as icy as if she'd been standing in a freezer. Her hair was matted and her lips and ears and nose were numb.

"It was wonderful," she gasped. "Like flying."

Deborah burst into laughter, jumped off, and slapped Cassie on the back. Then she helped Cassie off. Cassie couldn't stop shivering.

"Look over here," Deborah said, stepping over to the edge of the cliff.

Cassie looked. Far below, the dark water crashed and foamed around the rocks. It was a long way down.

But there was something beautiful, too. Over the vast gray curve of ocean, an almost half-full moon hung. It cast a long wavering trail of light along the water, pure silver on the darkness.

"It looks like a road," Cassie said softly, through chattering teeth. "Like you could ride on it."

She looked at Deborah quickly, not sure how the biker girl would take to such a fancy. But Deborah gave a short nod, her narrowed eyes still on the silver path.

"That would be the ultimate. Just ride till you fly straight off the edge. I guess that was what the old-time witches wanted," she said.

Cassie felt a warmth even through her shivering. Deborah felt what she herself had felt. And now Cassie understood why Deborah rode a motorcycle.

"We better go," Deborah said abruptly.

On the way back to the motorcycle Cassie stumbled, falling to one knee. She looked back and saw that she had tripped on a piece of brick or stone.

"I forgot to tell you; there used to be a house here," Deborah said. "It got torn down a long time ago, but there're some pieces of foundation left."

"I think I just found one," Cassie said.

Rubbing her knee, she was starting to get up when she noticed something beside the brick. It was darker than the soil it was resting on and yet it shone faintly in the moonlight.

She picked it up and found that it was smooth and surprisingly heavy. And it *did* shine; it reflected the moonlight like a black mirror.

"It's hematite," said Deborah, who'd come back to look. "It's a powerful stone—for iron-strength, Melanie says." She knelt down suddenly beside Cassie, tossing tangled hair out of her eyes. "Cassie! It's your working crystal."

A thrill which seemed to come from the stone rippled through Cassie. Holding the smooth piece of hematite was like holding an ice cube, but all the things that Melanie had said would happen when she found her own personal crystal were happening now. It fit her hand, it felt natural there. She liked the weight of it. It was *hers*.

Elated, she lifted her head to smile up at Deborah, and in the chilly moonlight Deborah smiled fiercely back.

It was when she was dropping Cassie off at Number Twelve that she said, "I heard you came to see Nick yesterday."

"Oh—um," Cassie said. That meeting with Nick in the garage seemed like centuries ago, not yesterday. "Uh, I didn't come to *see* him," she stammered. "I was just walking by . . ."

Deborah shrugged. "Anyway, I thought I'd tell you—he gets in bad moods sometimes. But that doesn't mean you should give up. Other times he's okay."

Cassie floundered, completely amazed. "Uh—well—I didn't mean—I mean, thanks, but I wasn't really . . ."

She couldn't find a way to finish, and Deborah wasn't waiting anyway. "Whatever. See you later. And don't lose that stone!" Dark hair flying, the biker girl zoomed off.

Up in her room, Cassie's legs felt weak from tension, and she was tired. But she lay in bed for a while and held the hematite on her palm, tilting it back and forth to watch the light slide over it. For iron-strength, she thought.

It wasn't like the chalcedony rose; it gave her no feeling of warmth and comfort. But then the chalcedony rose was all mixed up in her mind with Adam and his blue-gray eyes. Diana had the rose now, and Diana had Adam.

And Cassie had a stone which brought a strange coolness to her thoughts, a coolness that seemed to extend to her heart. For iron-strength, she thought again. She liked that.

"And so that's what Cassie believes, that each of the deaths—even Kori's—is connected to the skull, and to Puritan ways of killing people," Diana said. She looked around the circle of faces. "Now it's up to us to *do* something about it."

Cassie was watching Faye. She wanted to see the reaction in those hooded golden eyes when Diana explained about the dark energy that had escaped during the skull ceremony, killing Jeffrey. Sure enough, when Diana got to that part, Faye shot a glance at Cassie, but there was nothing apologetic or guilty about it. It was a look of conspiracy. *Only you and I know*, it said. *And I won't tell if you won't.*

I'm not that stupid, Cassie telegraphed back angrily, and Faye smiled.

It was Sunday night and they were all sitting on the beach. Diana hadn't been able to find out much from her own Book of Shadows about dealing with evil objects like the skull, and she was calling for everyone's help.

It was the first full meeting of the Circle in three weeks, since the day after Mr. Fogle had been found dead. Cassie scanned the faces above thick jackets and sweaters—even New Englanders had to bundle up in this weather—and wondered what was going on in each individual witch's head.

Melanie was grave and thoughtful as usual, as if she neither believed nor disbelieved Cassie's theory, but was willing to test it out scientifically. Laurel just looked appalled. Suzan was examining the stitching on her gloves. Deborah was scowling, unwilling to give up the idea that outsiders had killed Kori. Nick—well, who could tell what Nick thought? Sean was chewing his fingernails.

The Henderson brothers were agitated. For a terrible instant Cassie thought they were going to turn their energy on Adam, blame him for Kori's being killed. But then Doug spoke up.

"So how come we're still sittin' around talking? Let *me* have the skull—*I'll* take care of it," he said, teeth bared.

"Yeah—let Doug have it," Sean chimed in.

"It can't be destroyed, Doug," Melanie said patiently.

"Oh, yeah?" Chris said. "Put it in with a pipe bomb—"

"And nothing would happen. Crystal skulls

can't be destroyed, Doug," Melanie repeated. "That's in all the old lore. You wouldn't even scratch it."

"And there's no really safe place to store it," Diana said. "I might as well tell you all, I've got it buried somewhere, and yesterday I set up a spell to tell me if the place is disturbed. It's vital that the skull *stays buried*."

Cassie had a sick feeling in her stomach. Diana was looking around the group, focusing on Deborah, Faye, and the Hendersons. It would never occur to her to look at me, Cassie thought, and somehow this made her feel sicker than ever.

"Why can't we take it back to the island?" Suzan said, surprisingly, showing she was listening after all.

Adam, who had been sitting quietly, his fine, humorous face unusually moody, answered. "Because the island won't protect it anymore," he said. "Not since I took the skull."

"Sort of like one of those Egyptian tombs with a curse on it," said Laurel. "Once you break in, you can't undo what you've done."

Adam's lip quirked. "Right. And we're not strong enough to cast a new spell of protection that would hold it. This skull is *evil*," he said to all of them. "It's so evil that burying it in sand won't do anything but keep it from being activated at the moment. There's no way to purify it"—he looked at Laurel—"and no way to destroy it"—he looked at Doug and Chris—"and no place to keep it safe." He looked at Suzan.

"Then what do we do?" Deborah demanded, and Sean squeaked, "What do we *do*?"

"Forget about it?" Faye suggested with a lazy smile. Adam shot her a dark look. Diana intervened.

"Adam had the idea of searching for the dark energy again with a pendulum, seeing if there are any new trails," she said. She turned to Cassie. "What do you think?"

Cassie dug her fingernails into her palms. If they traced the dark energy and it led them straight back to Faye's house, the place where it had most recently escaped . . . Faye was looking at her sharply, wanting her to veto the suggestion. But Cassie had an idea.

"I think we should do it," she told Diana evenly.

Faye's stare turned menacing, furious. But there was nothing she could say.

Diana nodded. "All right. We may as well

start now. It's a long walk to the graveyard, so I thought we might try picking up the trail around here. We'll go out on Crowhaven Road and see if there's anything to follow."

Cassie could actually feel her chest quivering with the beating of her heart as they walked off the beach. She thrust one hand into her pocket to feel the cold, smooth piece of hematite. Iron-strength, that was what she needed right now.

"Are you crazy?" Faye hissed as they climbed the bluff and headed for the road. She caught Cassie's arm in a punishing grip, holding her back from the others. "Do you know where that trail *goes?*"

Cassie shook the arm off. "Trust me," she said shortly.

"*What?*"

Cassie whirled on the taller girl. "I said, trust me! I know what I'm doing—and you don't." And with that she began to climb again. Iron-strength, she thought dizzily, impressed with herself.

But she still found it hard to breathe when Diana stood out in the middle of Crowhaven Road—near Number Two, Deborah's house—and held up the peridot crystal.

Cassie watched it, feeling the concentration of all the minds around her. She waited for it to spin in circles.

It did—in the beginning. The chain twisted first one way and then the other, like a wound-up swing on a playground. But then, to Cassie's horror, it began to seesaw, pointing up and down Crowhaven Road. Down, the way they'd traveled the first time, the way that had eventually led to the cemetery, and up, toward the headland.

Toward Faye's.

Cassie's legs felt as if they were sinking into cotton as she followed the group. Faye had no trouble holding her back now. "I told you," she said vehemently out of the side of her mouth. "*Now* what, Cassie? If that trail leads to my house, I'm not going down alone."

Cassie clenched her teeth and choked out, "I thought we couldn't trace it at ground level. That energy came out through your bedroom ceiling on the second floor, and it was going straight up. I thought it would be too high to track."

"You obviously thought wrong," Faye hissed.

They were passing the vacant house at Number Three. They were passing Melanie's house. Laurel's house was in front of them; they were passing it. Faye's house was just ahead.

Cassie thought she actually might faint. She was almost unaware that she was clutching Faye's arm as hard as Faye was clutching hers. She waited for the peridot to turn aside and lead them all to Faye's doorstep.

But Diana was walking on.

Cassie felt a violent surge of relief—and of bewilderment. Where were they *going*? They were passing Number Seven, another vacant house. Passing the Hendersons', passing Adam's, passing Suzan's. They were passing Sean's—oh, my God, Cassie thought, we're not going to *my* house?

But they were passing Number Twelve as well. Diana was following the pendulum's swing, leading them out onto the point of the headland.

And there the crystal began to spin in circles again.

"What's going on?" Laurel said, looking around in astonishment. "What are we doing here?"

Adam and Diana were looking at each other. Then they both looked at Cassie, who came slowly forward from the rear of the group. Cassie shrugged at them.

"This is the place where Number Thirteen used to be," Diana said. "Right, Adam? The house that was torn down."

"I heard it burned down," Adam said. "Before we were born."

"No, it wasn't that long ago," said Melanie. "It was only about sixteen or seventeen years ago—that's what I heard. But before that it was vacant for centuries. Literally."

"How many centuries?" Cassie said, too loudly. For some reason she found her fingers clenched around the piece of hematite in her pocket.

The members of the coven turned to her, looking at her with eyes that seemed to shine slightly in the moonlight.

"About three," Melanie said. "This was Black John's house. Nobody ever lived in it after he died in 1696."

The hematite burned against Cassie's palm with icy fire.

O

ELEVEN

"This is all too weird for me," Laurel said, shivering.

"But what does it *tell* us?" Deborah challenged.

"It's another link to Black John," Adam said. "Other than that, nothing."

"So it's a dead end, like the cemetery," Faye said, looking pleased.

Cassie had the feeling they were wrong, but she couldn't explain why, so she kept her mouth shut. Something else was worrying her, worrying her terribly. The piece of hematite that right now felt as heavy as a bit of neutron star in her pocket . . . it had come from the ruins of Black John's house. It might even have belonged to him. Which meant that she had to tell Diana about it.

People were wandering around, breaking up into small groups. The meeting, for all intents and purposes, was over. Cassie took a deep breath and went to Diana.

"I didn't get a chance to talk to you earlier," she said. "But I wanted to tell you about something that happened yesterday."

"Cassie, you don't have to tell me. I know it wasn't like Faye said."

Cassie blinked, thrown off balance. "What did Faye say?"

"We don't even have to talk about it. I know it's not true."

"But what did she *say*?"

Diana looked uncomfortable. "She said— you were over at her house last night, playing— well, some kind of game."

"Pizza Man," Cassie said distinctly. When Diana stared at her, she explained, "Pizza Man He Delivers."

"I know what it's called," Diana said. She was scanning Cassie's face. "But I'm sure you would never . . ."

"*You're* sure? You can't be sure," Cassie cried. It was too much—Diana's blind insistence on her innocence. Didn't Diana realize that Cassie was bad, evil?

"Cassie, I *know* you. I know you wouldn't do anything like that."

Cassie was feeling more and more agitated. Something inside her was getting ready to snap. "Well, I was there. And I did do it. And"—she was getting close to the source of the anguish inside her—"you don't know what kind of things I would or wouldn't do. I've already done some things—"

"Cassie, calm down—"

Cassie reeled a step backward, stung. "I *am* calm. Don't tell me to calm down!"

"Cassie, what's wrong with you?"

"Nothing's wrong with me. I just want to be left alone!"

Diana's eyes sparked green. She was tired, Cassie knew, and anxious. And maybe she'd reached a snapping point, too. "All right," she said, with unaccustomed sharpness in her normally gentle voice. "I'll leave you alone, then."

"Fine," Cassie said, her throat swollen and her eyes stinging. She didn't want to fight with Diana—but all this anger and pain inside her had to go *somewhere*. She'd never known how awful it was to have people insist you were good, when you *weren't.*

Her fingers unclenched from the piece of hematite, and she left it in her pocket as she turned around and walked away. She stared down over the edge of the cliff at the swirling waves below.

Faye moved in beside her, bringing a scent of sweet, musky perfume. "Show it to me."

"Huh?"

"I want to see what's in your pocket that you've been holding on to like it might run away."

Cassie hesitated, then slowly drew the smooth, heavy stone out.

Still facing the ocean, Faye examined it. "A hematite crystal. That's rare." She held it up to the moonlight and chuckled. "Did Melanie ever tell you about some of hematite's more— unusual properties? No? Well, even though it looks black, if you cut it into thin slices, they're transparent and red. And the dust that comes off the stone turns the liquid that cools the cutting wheel as red as blood."

She gave the stone back to Cassie, who held it loosely, looking down at it. No matter where it came from, it was *her* crystal now. She'd known that from the moment she'd seen it. How could she give it up?

"I found it here, by the foundation of the house," she said dully.

Faye's eyebrows lifted. Then she collected herself. "Hm. Well—of course, anybody could have dropped it here in the past three hundred years."

A strange sense of excited relief filtered through Cassie. "Yes," she said. "Of course. Anybody could have." She put the crystal back in her pocket. Faye's hooded golden eyes were gleaming at her, and Cassie felt herself nod. She didn't have to give up the crystal after all.

Adam was calling people back into a group. "Just one thing before everybody leaves," he was saying. He seemed oblivious to the little drama that had been enacted between Cassie and Diana a few minutes earlier.

"I have an idea," he said, when the Club had gathered around again. "You know, I just realized that everything connected with the dark energy has led to death, to the dead. The cemetery; that ghost-shape Cassie and Deborah and Nick and I saw on the road; even this place—a ruined house built by a dead man. And—well, the weekend after next is Samhain."

There was a murmur from the group. Adam looked at Cassie and said, "You know, Halloween. All Saints' Eve, November Eve, whatever. But no matter what you call it, it's the night when the dead walk. And I know it might be dangerous, but I think we should do a ceremony, either here or at the cemetery, on Halloween. We'll see what we can call up." He turned to Diana. "What do you think?"

This time the response was silence. Diana looked concerned, Melanie doubtful, Sean openly scared. Doug and Chris were grinning their wild grins, and Deborah was nodding fiercely. Faye had her head cocked to one side, considering; Nick stood with his arms across his chest, stone-faced. But it was Laurel and Suzan who spoke up.

"But what about the *dance?*" Laurel said, and Suzan said, "Saturday night is the Halloween dance and I've already got my shoes."

"We always have a party on Halloween," Melanie explained to Cassie. "It's a big witch holiday. But this year Halloween falls on Saturday, and the school dance is the same night. Still," she said slowly, "I don't see why we couldn't do both. We could leave the dance around eleven thirty and still have plenty of time for a ceremony here."

"And I think it *should* be here," Diana said, "and not the graveyard. That's just *too* dangerous, and we might call up more than we bargained for."

Cassie thought of the shadowy form she and Adam had seen at the graveyard. A bit too belligerently, she asked, "What are we planning to do with whatever we *can* call up?"

"Talk to it," Adam said promptly. "In the old days people called up the spirits of the dead on Halloween and asked them questions. The spirits had to answer."

"It's the day when the veil between the worlds is the thinnest," Laurel clarified. "Dead people come back and visit their living relatives." She looked around the group. "I think we should do the ceremony."

There was agreement from the Circle, some of it hesitant, some enthusiastic. But everyone nodded.

"Right," Adam said. "Halloween night, then." Cassie thought it was unusual that he was taking over the job of coven leader this way, but then she looked at Diana. Diana looked as if she were holding some turmoil inside her tightly under control. For a moment

Cassie felt sorry for her, but then her own misery and conflict welled up. She left the meeting quickly, without speaking to Diana.

In the weeks before Halloween, the real cold set in, although the leaves were still bronze and crimson. Cassie's bedroom smelled of camphor because her grandmother had brought old quilts out of storage to pile on her bed. The last of the herbs had been gathered, and the house was decorated with autumn flowers, marigolds and purple asters. Every day after school Cassie found her grandmother in the kitchen, cooking oceans of applesauce to jar, until the whole house smelled of hot apple pulp and cinnamon and spices.

Pumpkins mysteriously appeared on everybody's back porch—but only Cassie and the Hendersons knew where they came from.

Things didn't get better with Diana.

A guilty part inside Cassie knew why. She didn't *want* to fight with Diana—but it was so much easier not having to worry about her all the time. If she wasn't always talking to Diana, wasn't over at Diana's house every day, she didn't have to think about how hurt Diana would be if Diana ever found out the truth.

The shameful secrets inside Cassie didn't rub her so much when Diana was at a distance.

So when Diana tried to make up, Cassie was polite but a little cool. A little—detached. And when Diana asked why Cassie was still mad, Cassie said she *wasn't* still mad, and why couldn't Diana just leave things alone? After that, Diana did.

Cassie felt as if a thin, hard shell were growing all over her.

She thought about what Deborah had said about Nick. *He gets in bad moods sometimes, but that doesn't mean you should give up.* Of course, there was no way Cassie could go back and ask Nick again. At least, there was no way the old Cassie could have. There seemed to be a new Cassie now, a stronger, harder one—at least on the outside. And she had to do *something*, because every night she thought about Adam and ached, and she was afraid of what might happen if she went to that dance unattached.

The day before Halloween she walked up to Nick's garage again.

The skeleton-car looked just the same. Its entire engine was out, resting on a sort of bottomless table made of pipes. Nick was underneath the table.

Cassie knew better than to ask him what he was doing this time. She saw him see her feet, saw his gaze travel up. Then he scooted out from under the table and stood up.

His dark hair was spiky with sweat, and he wiped his forehead with the back of a greasy hand. He didn't say anything, just stood there looking at her.

Cassie didn't give herself time to think. Focusing all her attention on an oil stain on his T-shirt, she said rapidly, "Are you going to the Halloween dance tomorrow?"

There was a long, long silence. Cassie stared at the oil stain while Nick stared at her face. She could smell rubber and warm metal as well as grease and a faint hint of gasoline. She felt as if she were hanging suspended in air.

Then Nick said, "No."

Everything came crashing down. Cassie felt it, and for some reason she was suddenly able to look Nick in the face.

"Oh," she said flatly. Oh, stupid, *stupid*, she was thinking. The new Cassie was as dumb as the old one. She should never have come here.

"I don't see why you want to know in the first place," Nick said. Then he added, "It's got something to do with Conant, doesn't it?"

Cassie tensed. "Adam? What are you talking about? What could my asking you to a dance have to do with Adam?" she said, but she could feel the blood rise to her face.

Nick was nodding. "I thought so. You've really got it bad. And you don't want him to know, so you're looking for a substitute, right? Or are you trying to make him jealous?"

Cassie's face was burning now, but hotter was the flame of rage and humiliation inside her. She wouldn't cry in front of Nick, she *wouldn't*.

"Sorry for bothering you," she said, and, feeling stiff and sore, she turned around to walk away.

"Wait a minute," Nick said. Cassie went on walking and reached the golden October sunlight. Her eyes were fixed on the fading scarlet leaves of a red maple across the street.

"Wait," Nick said again, closer. He'd followed her out. "What time do you want me to pick you up?" he said.

Cassie turned around and stared at him.

God, he *was* handsome, but so cold . . . even now he looked completely dispassionate, indifferent. The sun caught blue glints off his dark hair, and his face was like a perfectly carved ice sculpture.

"I don't want to go with you anymore," Cassie told him bleakly, and started away again.

He moved in front of her, blocking her without touching her. "I'm sorry I said the thing about trying to make Conant jealous. That was just . . ." He stopped and shrugged. "I didn't mean it. I don't know what's going on, and it's none of my business, anyway. But I'd like to go to the dance with you."

I'm hallucinating, Cassie thought. I've got to be. I thought I just heard Nick apologize . . . and then say he'd *like* to go with me. I must have a fever.

"So what time do you want me to pick you up?" Nick said again.

Cassie was having trouble breathing, so her voice was faint. "Um, about eight would be fine. We're all changing into our costumes at Suzan's house."

"Okay. I'll see you there."

On Halloween night, in Suzan's Greek Revival house, the girls of Crowhaven Road prepared themselves. This night was different than the evening of the Homecoming dance. For one thing, Cassie knew what she was doing now. Suzan had taught her how to do her own makeup, in exchange for Cassie helping Suzan with her costume.

They'd all taken baths with fresh sage leaves; Laurel's orders, for enhancing their psychic powers. Cassie had also washed in milk of roses—rosewater and oil of sweet almonds—for softening her skin and to smell nice. Cassie's grandmother had helped her plan and make her costume, which consisted mainly of panels of thin gauze.

When she was finished that night, Cassie looked in Suzan's mirror and saw a girl slender as a candle flame, dressed in something like mist, with an elusive, glancing beauty. The girl had hair like smoky topaz curling around a delicate face, and as Cassie watched, rosy shadows bloomed on her pale skin.

She looked soft and touchable and sensuous, but that was all right, because she would be with Nick. Cassie dabbed perfume behind her ears—not magnet oil but simply attar of roses—and tossed her scented hair back. Well, there was a certain wistfulness in the girl's wildflower-blue eyes, but that couldn't be helped. Nothing was going to cure that, ever.

She wasn't wearing any crystal to allure, only the hematite for iron-strength in a pouch under her costume.

"What are you?" Deborah said, looking into the mirror over her shoulder.

"I'm a muse. It's an old-time Greek thing; my grandmother showed it to me in a book. They weren't goddesses, just sort of divine guides. They inspired people with creativity," Cassie said. She looked at herself uncertainly. "I guess I'm Calliope; she was muse of poetry. The others were muses of history and stuff."

Melanie spoke up. "Witches believe that there was only one muse before they got split up into nine. She was the spirit of the arts, all of them. So maybe tonight you're her."

Cassie turned to look at their costumes. Deborah was a rocker, all silver bangles, studs, and black leather. Melanie was Sophia, the biblical spirit of wisdom, with a sheer veil over her face and a wreath of silver stars in her hair.

Suzan had taken Cassie's suggestion and dressed up as Aphrodite, goddess of love. Cassie had gotten the idea from Diana's prints and her grandmother's book of Greek myths. "Aphrodite was supposed to be born from the sea," she said now. "That's the reason for all the shells."

Suzan's hair was loose around her shoulders,

and her robe was the color of sea foam. Iridescent sequins, seed pearls, and tiny shells decorated the mask she held in her hand.

Laurel was a fairy. "A *nature* spirit," she said, pivoting to show long, curving dragonfly wings. She was wearing a garland of leaves and silk flowers on her head.

"Everyone looks great," a soft voice said, and Cassie turned and caught her breath. Diana wasn't even dressed up, or at least she was only wearing her ceremonial costume, the one she wore at Circles. But she appeared to be wreathed in her own light and she was beautiful beyond description.

Laurel spoke quietly in Cassie's ear. "She's not making fun of it or anything, you know. Halloween's our most magical holiday of the year. She's honoring it."

"Oh," Cassie murmured. Her eyes slid to Faye.

Faye, she guessed, was a witch. The kind that guys were afraid of. She was wearing a sleeveless black dress, like a parody of the white shift Diana wore at meetings of the Circle. It was slit up both sides to the hip, and cut to show every curve. The material shimmered like silk when she walked.

There are going to be some hearts broken at the dance tonight, Cassie thought.

Downstairs, the doorbell rang, and the girls all went down in their fluttering draperies and rippling gowns to meet the guys. The Club was going to this dance in a group, as they planned to leave in a group at eleven thirty.

Nick was Cassie's date, but in that first moment all she could see was Adam. He was amazing. The branched ends of stag antlers sprouted from a crown of oak leaves on his head, and he was wearing a mask of oak leaves and acorns.

"He's Herne, the horned god," Melanie said. "Sort of like Pan, you know, a nature god. He's god of animals, too—that's why he gets to take Raj with him."

Raj *was* there, trying to thrust his nose forward to give Cassie one of his embarrassingly warm greetings. Adam—or Herne; it unnerved Cassie how natural he looked with the horns and the oak leaves—held the dog back.

The other girls were laughing at the guys' costumes. "Sean," Laurel said, "you're skinny enough without showing all your bones." He was dressed as a skeleton.

Chris and Doug had strange symbols painted

on their faces: black and red triangles, yellow lightning bolts. Their long hair was even more disheveled than usual. "We're Zax," they said, and everyone said, "*Who?*"

Chris answered: "Zax the magician. He pulls cigarettes out of the air."

"It's from some science-fiction show they saw once," Suzan explained finally.

Faye's slow, lazy voice broke in. "And just what are you supposed to be, Nick? The Man in Black?"

Cassie looked at Nick for the first time. He wasn't wearing a costume, just black jeans and a black pullover sweater. He looked very handsome, very cool.

"I'm supposed to be *her* date," he said calmly, and without another look at Faye he held out his hand to Cassie.

Faye can't mind, Cassie told herself as they walked to the line of cars outside. Faye doesn't want him anymore; she shouldn't care who he goes with. But there was a thin coil of uneasiness in her stomach as she let Nick guide her to the Armstrong car. Deborah and Laurel got in the back.

On the porches around them, jack-o'-lanterns had fiery grins and dancing flames for eyes. It was a crystal moonlit night.

"A haunted night," Laurel said from the backseat. "Tonight spirits gather at all the windows and doors, looking in. We always put a white candle in the window to guide them."

"Or a plate of food to feed them, so they don't try to come inside," Deborah said in a hollow voice.

Cassie laughed, but there was a slightly false note in the laughter. She didn't want spirits looking in her windows. And as for what Laurel had said two weeks ago, about dead relatives coming back to visit the living—well, Cassie didn't want that, either. She didn't know any of her dead relatives, except her father, and he probably wasn't really dead. No, on the whole, she'd rather just leave all dead people alone.

But the Circle was planning to do just the opposite tonight.

The gym was decorated with owls, bats, and witches flying across giant yellow moons. Black and orange crepe paper was wound around the girders and streamed from the basketball hoops. There were dancing skeletons, spitting cats with arched backs, and surprised-looking ghosts on the walls.

It was all so fun and harmless. The ordinary students who'd come to dance and masquerade and drink purple poison punch had no idea of the real darkness that lurked outside. Even the ones who hated the Club didn't know the full truth.

Diana and Adam arrived together, making what must have been the most impressive entrance New Salem High School had ever seen. Diana, in her simple white shift, with her bare throat and arms looking as fresh as baby's skin, and her aureole of shining hair falling down her back, looked like a shaft of moonlight that had somehow wandered accidentally into the gym.

And Adam—Adam always had a presence, a way of innately commanding respect from anyone smart enough really to look at him. Tonight, as Herne, he was more arresting than ever. He seemed to *be* the forest god, perilous and mischievous, awe-inspiring but not unkind. Above all, he looked wild. There was nothing domesticated about him; he belonged in the open spaces, running underneath the stars. Raj stayed beside him, looking more like a wolf than a dog, and none of the chaperons said a word of objection.

"You know what happens tonight," a voice murmured, breath warm on Cassie's neck.

Cassie said, "What, Faye?" without turning around.

"Well, the coven leaders who represent the goddess Diana and the horned god have to make an alliance. They have to . . ." Faye paused delicately. ". . . merge, shall we say? To represent the union of male and female principals."

"You mean they . . . ?"

"It can be done symbolically," Faye said blandly. "But somehow I don't think Adam and Diana will be satisfied with symbolism, do you?"

TWELVE

Cassie stood petrified. Her heart was going like a trip-hammer, but that was the only part of her capable of motion.

Adam and Diana . . . they *couldn't*. Only, of course, they could. Diana was laughing up at Adam now, tossing her straight, shining hair back. And although Cassie couldn't see Adam's eyes behind the mask, his lips were smiling.

Cassie turned, almost blundering into Nick, who was bringing her some punch, and rushed off into the dimness.

She found a dark corner under a Chinese lantern that had gone out. Shielded by a curtain of black and orange streamers, she stood there, trying to get hold of herself, trying not to see the pictures her mind was showing her.

The next thing she knew, she could smell wood smoke and ocean breeze, along with a faint, indefinable scent of animal and oak leaves. Adam.

"Cassie," he said. Just that, as if Herne were calling her in her dreams, inviting her to throw off the covers in the middle of the night and come dancing in the autumn leaves.

And then, in a more ordinary voice, he said quietly, "Cassie, are you okay? Diana says—"

"What?" Cassie demanded, in a way that would have been fierce if her voice hadn't been trembling.

"She's just worried that you're not all right."

"I'm all right!" Cassie was struggling not to let the tears escape. "And anyway—I'm tired of people talking about me behind my back. Faye says, Diana says—I'm *tired* of it."

He took both her cold hands in his. "I think," he said in a subdued voice, "that you're just tired, period."

I am, Cassie thought. I'm tired of having secrets. And I'm tired of fighting. If I'm already evil, what's the point of fighting?

Just at the moment, to think was to act.

205

Before she knew what she was doing, her hands had turned inside Adam's, so that her fingers were clasping his. *Not by word or look or deed,* what a laugh, she thought. We've already broken it a thousand times. Why not really break it? That way at least she would have something concrete to feel bad about. That way Diana wouldn't have him first.

That was the crux of it. Diana might have everything else, but she wouldn't have Adam first.

I could do it, Cassie thought. Suddenly, her mind was working coolly and rationally, far removed from all the twisted pain in her chest. Adam was vulnerable to her because he was honorable, because he would never dream of her scheming to get him.

If she started to cry right now . . . If she got him close enough to hold her, then relaxed against him, making herself soft in his arms . . . If she laid her head on his shoulder so that he could smell her hair . . . If she sighed and let her head fall back . . . would he be able to resist kissing her?

Cassie didn't think so.

There were places darker than this corner. Safe places in the school. The home-ec room with the lock anyone could pick, the storage compartment where the gymnastics mats were kept. If Adam kissed her and she kissed him back, could anything stop them from going there?

Cassie didn't think so.

And Diana, sweet *stupid* innocent Diana, would never know the difference. If Adam said he'd had to take Cassie for a walk to calm her down, Diana would believe him.

No, there was nothing to stop Cassie and Adam . . . except the oath. How did it go again? *Fire burn me, air smother me, earth swallow me, water cover my grave.* Cassie wasn't afraid of that. Fire was burning her body already, and air was smothering her—she couldn't breathe. There was nothing to stop her. She leaned in closer to Adam, head drooping like a flower on a slender stem, feeling the first easy tears come. She heard the catch in her breath, and felt his fingers tighten on hers in concern, and awareness.

"Cassie—God . . ." he whispered.

A fierce rush of triumph swept through Cassie. He couldn't help himself. It was going to happen. *Oak and holly, leaf and briar/ Touch him with the secret fire . . .*

What was she *doing*?

Using magic on *Adam*? Snaring him with words that had come from some deep well of knowledge within herself? It was wrong, dishonorable, and not just because members of the Club didn't work spells on each other unasked.

It was wrong because of Diana.

Diana, who'd been Cassie's friend when no one else would speak to her. Who'd championed her against Faye and the whole school. Even if Cassie couldn't deal with being close to Diana right now, the memory of Diana was like a star shining in her mind. If she betrayed that, she betrayed everything that meant anything.

Evil or not, Cassie couldn't do it.

She extracted her hands from Adam's strong fingers.

"I'm all right," she said, her voice soft and weak, all its bones crushed.

He was trying to get hold of her hands again. That was the problem with magic, you couldn't always stop what you'd started. "Adam, really," she said. Then, desperately, she added, "Diana's waiting."

Saying Diana's name helped. He stood for a

moment, then escorted her back, Herne bringing a wayward nymph home to the Circle. Cassie went over to Laurel for safety; Nick was nowhere in sight. Well, she didn't blame him.

Diana was talking to Sally Waltman, who was there and looking hard as nails, despite the loss of Jeffrey. That left Adam and Cassie with Laurel and Melanie and their dates, and Sean and Deborah. A merry group of witches. Next to them was a group of outsiders.

A slow dance was starting. The group of outsiders broke up, moving onto the dance floor. All except one.

That one remained standing there, isolated, on the fringe of the Club. She was a junior Cassie vaguely recognized from French class, a shy girl, not beautiful, but not ugly, either. Right now she was trying to pretend that she didn't mind being abandoned, that she didn't care.

Cassie's heart went out to her. Poor girl. Once, Cassie had been just like her.

"Want to dance?" It was Adam's voice, warm and friendly— but he wasn't talking to Cassie, he was talking to the outsider girl. Her face lit up, and she went happily with him out onto the floor, the scales of her mermaid costume flashing and twinkling. Cassie watched them go with a pang.

But not of jealousy. Of love—and respect.

"The parfit gentil knight," Melanie said.

"What?" said Cassie.

"It's from Chaucer. We learned it in British lit class. That's what Adam is, the perfect gentle knight," Melanie explained.

Cassie thought about this for a while. Then she turned to Sean. "Hey, skinny, want to shake your bones?" she said.

Sean's face lit up.

Well, Cassie thought as she and Sean began swaying to the music, one thing was for sure: This dance *wasn't* anything like the last one. With Adam, the gym had seemed a place of beauty and enchantment. Now all she saw were paper cutouts and naked pipes overhead. At least Sean-the-Day-Glo-skeleton didn't try to pull her in too close.

Afterward, other guys approached her, but Cassie made a beeline for Nick, who'd rematerialized, and hid behind him. At least this part of her plan worked—the other guys retreated. It was strange to be something everybody wanted and couldn't have. Nick didn't ask her why she'd rushed off, and she didn't ask him where he'd disappeared to.

They danced a few times. Nick didn't try to kiss her.

And then it was time to leave. After saying good-bye to their bewildered, slightly indignant dates, the members of the Club gathered at the exit, and not even the strawberry-blond goddess Aphrodite was late. Even the two identical Zaxes, their slanted blue-green eyes sparkling, were waiting outside the door. Then they all started off into the darkness. The moon had set, but the stars seemed to be on fire.

It was cold on the point of the headland. They sat on bits of the foundation of the razed house, while Deborah and Faye built a bonfire in the center. Other people were bringing provisions out of the cars. Cassie had expected everyone to be solemn, but the Circle was in a party mood, excited by the night, laughing and joking, defying the danger of what they were going to do in an hour or so. Cassie found herself enjoying the celebration, not thinking about the future.

There was lots of food. Dried pumpkin seeds ("Without *salt*," Laurel said), pumpkin bread and gingerbread baked by Diana, boxes of

211

chocolate- and orange-frosted doughnuts from Adam, a bowl of mixed Halloween candy provided by Suzan, soft drinks and spiced cider, and a large paper bag of Chris's that rattled.

"Nuts! Yeah! For virility!" Doug yelled to the other guys, with an uncouth gesture.

"Hazelnuts symbolize wisdom," Melanie said patiently, but the Henderson brothers just sneered.

And there were apples: winesaps, greenings, macintoshes. "Apples for love and death," Diana said. "Especially at Halloween. Did you know they were sacred to the goddess Hera?"

"Did you know the seeds contain cyanide?" Faye added, smiling oddly. She'd been smiling oddly at Cassie ever since Cassie had emerged from behind the streamer curtain with Adam at the dance. Now, leaning over to take a piece of gingerbread, she murmured in Cassie's ear, "What happened back there when he followed you? Did you blow your chance?"

"It isn't nice to fool around with guys who're taken," Cassie whispered tiredly, as if explaining to a five-year-old.

Faye chuckled. "Nice? Is that what you want for your epitaph? 'Here lies Cassie. She was . . . nice'?"

Cassie turned her head away.

"I know an apple spell," Laurel was saying to the group. "You peel an apple in one long spiral, then throw the peel over your shoulder, and if it doesn't break, it forms the initial of your true love."

They tried this, without much success. The peelings kept breaking, Suzan cut herself on Deborah's knife, and when Diana did manage to throw a peeling over her shoulder, it only formed a spiral.

"Well, that's sacred to the goddess at least," Laurel said, frowning. "Or to the Horned One," she added mischievously, looking at Adam.

Cassie had been deliberately breaking her apple peels; the whole fortune-telling thing made her uneasy. And not just because Melanie mentioned cheerfully, "They used to execute witches for this kind of divination on Halloween."

"I've got another one," Laurel said. "You throw a nut in the fire, say a pair of names, and see what happens. Like Suzan and David Downey," she added impishly. "If the nut pops, they're meant for each other. If it doesn't, they're doomed."

"If he loves me, pop and fly; if he hates me, burn and die!" Suzan quoted dramatically as Laurel tossed a hazelnut in. The round little nut just sizzled.

"Laurel and Doug," Chris snickered, throwing in another.

"Chris and Sally Waltman!" Doug countered.

"Cassie and Nick!"

Deborah tossed that one in, grinning, but Faye was noticeably unsmiling.

"Adam . . ." she said, holding a nut up high between long red nails and waiting until she had everyone's attention. Cassie stared at her, poised on the edge of her brick. ". . . and Diana," Faye said finally, and flicked the hazelnut into the flames.

Cassie, mesmerized, watched the nut where it lay on glowing embers. She didn't want to look at it; she had to.

"There are lots of other Halloween traditions," Laurel was going on. "It's time to remember old people, people who're coming to the winter of their lives—or that's what my Granny Quincey says."

Cassie was still staring at that one hazelnut. It seemed to be jiggling—but was it going to pop?

"It's getting late," Adam said. "Don't you think we should get started?"

Diana brushed pumpkin-bread crumbs off her hands and stood. "Yes."

Cassie only took her eyes off the fire for an instant, but in that instant, there was a sound like gunfire. Two or three nuts had exploded at once, and when Cassie looked back she couldn't see the one Faye had thrown. It had popped—or she'd lost track of it. She couldn't tell which.

A heartbeat later it flashed through her mind to wonder about Deborah's nut—for Cassie and Nick. But she couldn't tell what had become of that one, either.

"All right, now," Diana said. "This is going to be a different kind of Circle. It's going to be more powerful than anything we've ever used before, because we need more protection than we've ever needed before. And it's going to take everybody's help." She followed this with an earnest glance at Faye, who replied with a look of utmost innocence.

Cassie watched Diana draw a circle inside the ruined foundation with her black-handled knife. The bonfire was at the center. Everyone was serious now, their eyes following the path of the knife as it cut through the soil, making an almost perfect ring with a single gap at the northeast corner.

"Everyone get inside, and then I'll close it," Diana said. They all filed inside and sat along the inner perimeter of the ring. Only Raj was left on the outside, watching anxiously and whining a little in his throat.

"After this," Diana said, closing the gap with a sweep of the knife, "no one leaves the protection of the circle. What we're summoning up inside will be dangerous, but what'll be hanging around outside will be even worse."

"How dangerous?" Sean said nervously. "What's inside, I mean."

"We'll be safe as long as we don't go near the fire or touch it," Diana said. "No matter how strong a spirit it is, it won't be able to part from the fire we use to summon it. All right," she added briskly, "now I'm going to call on the Watchtower of the East. Powers of Air, protect us!"

Standing facing the dark eastern sky and ocean, Diana held a burning stick of incense and blew it eastward across the circle. "Think of air!" she told the coven members, and at once Cassie not only thought of it, but felt it, heard it. It started as a gentle breeze blowing from the east, but then it began to gust. It became a blast, a roaring wind beating in their faces, blowing Diana's long hair backward like a banner. And then it diverted, flowing around the circumference of the circle, enclosing them.

Diana took a burning stick out of the fire and moved to stand in front of Cassie, who was seated at the southernmost edge of the circle. Waving the stick over Cassie's head, she said, "Now I'm calling on the Watchtower of the South. Powers of Fire, protect us!"

She didn't need to say, *think of fire*. Cassie could already feel the heat radiating on her back, could picture the pillar of flame bursting up behind her. It raced around like sparks across gunpowder, to form a circle of wildfire just outside the circle of wind.

It's not real, Cassie reminded herself. They're just symbols we're visualizing. But they were awfully concrete-looking symbols.

Diana moved again. Dipping her fingers in a paper cup, she sprinkled water across the western perimeter, between Sean and Deborah. "I'm calling on the Watchtower of the West. Powers of Water, protect us!"

It surged up, a phantom glass-green wave, cresting higher and higher. The swell flowed around to encompass the circle with a wall of water.

Lastly, Diana moved north, facing Adam and scattering salt across the northern line. "Watchtower of the North," she said, in a voice that wavered slightly and showed how much this was taking out of her. "Powers of Earth, protect us!"

The ground rumbled beneath them.

It caught Cassie off guard, and the rest of the group was even more startled than she was. They weren't used to earthquakes here in New England, but Cassie was a native Californian. She saw that Sean was about to jump up.

"Deborah, get Sean!" she cried.

In an instant, the biker girl had grabbed Sean and was forcibly holding him from running. The tremors became more and more violent— and then with a sound like a thunderclap, the ground split. A chasm opened all around the circle, spewing up a strong, sulfurous smell.

It isn't real. It isn't real, Cassie reminded herself. But surrounding her she saw the phantoms of the four elements Diana had invoked, layered one after another. A circle of raging wind, then a ring of fire, then a wall of seawater, and finally a chasm in the earth. Nothing from the outside could pass those boundaries—and Cassie wouldn't like to bet on anything from the inside getting out safely, either.

Shakily, Diana walked over to sit down in her place between Nick and Faye. "Okay," she said, almost in a whisper. "Now we all concentrate on the fire. Look into it and let the night do the rest. Let's see if anything comes to talk to us."

Cassie's eyes shifted to Melanie, beside her. "But if we're protected from everything outside, who's going to be able to come talk to us?" she murmured.

"Something from *here*," Melanie whispered back, looking down at the barren earth inside the circle. Inside the foundations of the house.

"Oh."

Cassie gazed into the flames, trying to clear her mind, to be open to whatever might be trying to cross the veil between the invisible world and this one. Tonight was the night, and now was the time.

The fire began smoking.

Just a little at first, as if the wood were damp.

But then the smoke got darker—still transparent, but blacker. It streamed upward and hung in a cloudy mass above the bonfire.

Then it began to change.

It was twisting, swelling, like thunderheads rolling together. As Cassie stared, her breath clogging in her throat, it began to mold itself, to form a shape.

A man-shape.

It seemed to develop from the top down, and it was wearing old-fashioned clothes, like something out of a history book. A hat with a high crown and a stiff brim. A cloak or cape which hung down from broad shoulders, and a wide, severe linen collar. Breeches tied below the knees. Cassie thought she could make out square-toed shoes, but at times the lower legs just dwindled into the smoke of the fire. One thing she noticed, the smoke never actually detached from the fire, it always remained connected by a thin trail.

The figure floated there motionless except for eddies within itself.

Then it drifted toward Cassie.

She was the one who seemed to be facing it straight on. A sudden thought came into her mind. When Adam had first taken the crystal skull out of his backpack on the beach, it had seemed to be looking directly at her. And again—at the skull ceremony, she remembered. When Diana had pulled the cloth off the skull then, those hollow eyesockets had seemed to be staring right into Cassie's eyes.

Now this thing was staring at her in the same way.

"We should ask it a question," Melanie said, but even her usually calm voice was unsteady. There was a feeling of menace about the cloudy shape, of evil. Like the dark energy inside the skull, only stronger. More immediate.

Who are you? thought Cassie, but her tongue was frozen, and anyway, she didn't need to ask. There was no doubt at all in her mind who the shape in front of her was.

Black John.

Then came Diana's voice, clear and carefully calm. "We've invited you here because we've found something of yours," she said. "We need to know how to control it. Will you talk to us?"

There was no answer. Cassie thought the thing was moving closer to her—but maybe it was just an illusion.

"There are terrible things going on," Adam

said. "They have to be stopped."

No illusion. It was coming closer.

"Are *you* controlling the dark energy?" Melanie asked abruptly, and Laurel's voice blended with hers: "You're dead! You've got no right to be interfering with the living."

"What's your problem, anyway?" Deborah demanded.

Too fast, Cassie thought. Too many people asking questions. The shape was drifting steadily closer. Cassie felt paralyzed, as if she were in danger that no one else saw.

"Who killed Kori?" Doug Henderson was snarling.

"Why did the dark energy lead us to the cemetery?" Deborah jumped in.

"And what happened to Jeffrey?" Suzan added.

The trail of smoke connecting the shape to the fire was stretched out thin, and the shape was right in front of Cassie. She was afraid to look into that cloudy, indistinct face, but she had to. In its contours she thought she could recognize the face she'd glimpsed inside the crystal skull.

Get up, Cassie.

The words weren't real words, they were in

her mind. And they had some power over her. Cassie felt herself shift position, begin to rise.

Come with me, Cassie.

The others were still asking questions, and dimly Cassie could hear barking far away. But much louder was the voice in her mind.

Cassie, come.

She got to her feet. The swirling darkness seemed to be less transparent now. More solid. It was reaching out a formless hand.

Cassie reached out with her own hand to take it.

THIRTEEN

"Cassie, no!"

Later Cassie would realize it was Diana who had shouted. At the time the words came to her only through a fog, and they sounded slow and dragging. Meaningless, like the continued mad barking that was going on somewhere far away. Cassie's fingertips brushed the transparent black fingertips before her.

Instantly, she felt a jolt like the thrill that the hematite had given her. She looked up, shocked, from her own hand to the smoky, swirling face, and she *recognized* it—

Then everything shattered.

There was a great splash and icy-cold drops of water splattered Cassie from head to foot.

At the same instant there was the hissing sound of red-hot embers being suddenly drenched. The smoky man-thing changed, dwindling, dissolving, as if it were being sucked back into the fire. A fire that now was nothing more than a sodden black mess of charred sticks.

Adam was standing on the other side of the circle, holding the cooler, whose contents had doused the fire. Raj was behind him, hair bristling, lips skinned back from his teeth.

Cassie stared from her own outstretched hand to Adam's wide eyes. She swayed. Then everything seemed to go soft and gray around her, and she fainted.

"You're safe now. Just lie still." The voice seemed to come from a great distance, but it had a note of gentle authority. Diana, Cassie thought vaguely, and a great longing swept over her. She wanted to hold Diana's hand, but it was too much trouble to move or try to open her eyes.

"Here's the lavender water," came another voice, lighter and more hasty. Laurel. "You dab it on, like this . . ."

Cassie felt a coolness on her forehead and wrists. A sweet, clean smell cleared her head a little.

She could hear other voices now. ". . . maybe, but I still don't know how the hell Adam did it. I couldn't move—felt like I was frozen." That was Deborah.

"Me, too! Like I was stuck to the ground." That was Sean.

"Adam, will you please sit down now so Laurel can look at you? *Please?* You're hurt." That was Melanie, and suddenly Cassie could open her eyes. She sat up and a cool damp cloth fell off her forehead into her lap.

"No, no—Cassie, lie still," Diana said, trying to push her back down. Cassie was staring at Adam.

His wonderful unruly hair was blown every which way. His skin was reddened, like a skier with a bad case of windburn, and his clothes looked askew and damp. "I'm all right," he was saying to Melanie, who was trying to sit him in a chair.

"What happened? Where are we?" Cassie said. She was lying on a couch in a shabby living room she knew she should recognize, but she felt very confused.

"We brought you to Laurel's house," said Diana. "We didn't want to scare your mom and grandma. You fainted. But Adam saved your life."

"He went *through* the four circles of

protection," Suzan said, with a distinct note of awe in her voice.

"Stupid," Deborah commented. "But impressive."

And then came Faye's lazy drawl: "I think it was a tremendously devoted thing to do."

There was a startled pause. Then Laurel said, "Oh, well, you know Adam and duty. I guess he *is* devoted to it."

"*I* would've done it—so would Doug—if we could've got up," Chris insisted.

"And if you could've thought of it—which you couldn't," Nick said dryly and a little grimly. His expression was dark.

Cassie was watching as Laurel dabbed with a damp towel at Adam's face and hands. "This is aloe and willow bark," Laurel explained. "It should keep the burns from getting worse."

"Cassie," Diana said gently, "do you remember what happened before you fainted?"

"Uh . . . you guys were asking questions—too many questions. And then—I don't know, this voice started talking in my head. That thing was staring at me . . ." Cassie had a sudden thought. "Diana—at the skull ceremony in your garage, you know how you had the skull under a cloth?" Diana nodded. "Did you have it facing any particular way under the cloth?"

Diana looked startled. "Actually, there was something about that that worried me. I put the skull facing the place where I'd sit in the circle—but when I took the cloth off, it was facing the other way."

"It was facing *me*," Cassie said. "Which means either somebody moved it or . . . it moved itself." They were looking at each other, both puzzled and uneasy, but *communicating*. Cassie felt closer to Diana than she had in weeks. Now was the time to make up, she thought.

"Diana," she began, but just then she noticed something. Adam's mask of horns and oak leaves was sitting on a chair beside Diana, and one of Diana's slender hands was resting on it, caressing it as if for comfort. It was an unconscious gesture—and a completely revealing one. A bolt of resentment shot through Cassie's heart. Herne and the goddess Diana—they *belonged* together, right? And Diana knew it. Later tonight they'd probably perform that little ceremony Faye had been talking about.

Cassie looked up and found Faye looking at her, golden eyes hooded and ironic. Faye smiled faintly.

"What is it?" Diana was saying. "Cassie?"

"Nothing." Cassie stared down at the threadbare violet rug on the hardwood floor. "Nothing. I feel all right now," she added. It was true, the disorientation was almost gone. But the memory of that smoky face stayed with her.

"What an ending to our Halloween," Laurel said.

"We should have stayed at the dance," said Suzan, sitting back and crossing her legs. "We didn't learn anything—*and* Cassie got hurt," she added, after a moment's thought.

"But we did learn something. We learned that Black John's ghost is still around—and it's malevolent," Adam said. "It certainly wouldn't answer any of our questions."

"And it's strong," Diana said. "Strong enough to influence all of us, to keep us from moving." She looked at Cassie. "Except Cassie. I wonder why."

Cassie felt a flash of discomfort, and she shrugged.

"It doesn't matter how strong it is," Melanie said. "Halloween's over in a few hours, and after that it won't have any power."

"But we still don't know any more about the skull. Or about Kori," Doug said, unusually serious.

"And *I* don't think we even know that Black John is—how did you put it, Adam? Malevolent," came Faye's husky slow voice. "Maybe he just didn't feel like talking."

"Oh, don't be ridiculous," began Laurel.

Before an argument could break out, Diana said, "Look, it's late, and we're all tired. We're not going to get anything solved tonight. If Cassie really is okay, I think we should all go home and get some rest."

There was a pause, and then nods of agreement.

"We can talk about it at school—or at Nick's birthday," Laurel said.

"I'll take Cassie home," Nick said at the door.

Cassie glanced at him quickly. He hadn't said much while she'd been lying on the couch—but he'd *been* there. He'd come along with the rest of them to make sure she was all right.

"Then Deborah can come with me," Melanie said. "She rode in with you, right?"

"Can you drive me, too? I really am tired,"

Diana said, and Melanie nodded easily.

Cassie scarcely noticed the rest of the good-byes. What she was noticing was that Adam was leaving in his Jeep Cherokee, heading north, and Diana was going with Melanie and Deborah, going south.

No Herne-and-Diana ceremony *tonight*, Cassie thought, and a wash of relief went through her. Relief—and a ripple of mean gladness. It was wrong, it was bad—but she felt it.

Just as she got into Nick's car, she saw Faye smiling at her with raised eyebrows, and before she knew it, Cassie had smiled back.

The next day when Cassie stepped out of her house she stopped in shock. The sugar-maple trees across the street had changed. The blazing autumn colors that had reminded her of fire were gone. So were the leaves. Every branch was bare.

It looked like a Halloween skeleton.

"Nick won't let us do much for his birthday tomorrow," Laurel said. "I wish we could give him a *real* surprise party."

Deborah snorted. "He'd walk right out."

"I know. Well, we'll try to think of something he won't think is too infantile. And"—Laurel brightened—"we can make up for it on the other birthdays."

"What other birthdays?" Cassie said.

All the girls of the Club looked at her. They were sitting in the back room of the cafeteria, having a special conference while the guys kept Nick away.

"You mean you don't *know* about the birthday season?" Suzan asked in disbelief. "Diana didn't tell you?"

Diana opened her mouth and then shut it again. Cassie guessed she didn't know how to say that she and Cassie didn't talk that much anymore, at least not in private.

"Let's see if I can keep it straight," Faye said with a low chuckle, eyes on the ceiling. She began to count on fingers tipped with long, gleaming scarlet nails. "Nick's is November third. Adam's is November fifth. Melanie's is November seventh. Mine—and oh, yes, Diana's, too—is November tenth . . ."

"Are you *kidding*?" Cassie broke in.

Laurel shook her head as Faye went relentlessly on. "Chris and Doug's is November seventeenth, Suzan's is the twenty-fourth, and Deborah's is the twenty-eighth. Laurel's is, um . . ."

"December first," Laurel said. "And Sean's is December third, and that's it."

"But that's . . ." Cassie's voice trailed off. She couldn't believe it. Nick was only a month older than Sean? And *all* the witch kids were eight or nine months older than she was? "But you and Sean are juniors, like me," she said to Laurel. "And my birthday's July twenty-third."

"We just missed the cutoff date," Laurel said. "Everybody born after November thirtieth has to wait another year for school. So we had to watch everybody else go off to kindergarten while we stayed home." She wiped away imaginary tears.

"But that's still . . ." Cassie couldn't express herself. "Don't you think that's pretty incredible? All of you guys being born within a month of each other!"

Suzan dimpled wickedly. "It was a very wet April that year. Our parents all stayed inside."

"It *seems* odd, I admit," Melanie said. "But the fact is that most of our parents got married the spring before. So it really isn't that surprising."

"But . . ." Cassie still thought it *was* surprising, although clearly all the members of the Club were so used to it they didn't wonder about it anymore. And why don't I fit in the pattern? she thought. I guess it's because I'm half outsider. She shrugged. Melanie was probably right; anyway, there was no point in worrying. She let the subject drop and they went back to planning Nick's party.

They finally decided to combine all the birthdays for that first week—Nick's, Adam's, and Melanie's—and hold the party on Saturday, November seventh.

"*And*," Laurel said, when they explained their plan to the boys, "this one is going to be *really* different. Don't ask now—it's going to be *unique*."

"Uh, it's not some health-food kind of thing, is it?" Doug said, looking suspicious.

The girls looked at each other and stifled laughter. "Well—it *is* healthy—or at least some people think so," Melanie said. "You'll just have to come and see."

"But we'll freeze to death," Sean said, horrified.

"Not with this," Laurel laughed. She held up a thermos.

234

"Laurel." Adam was having a hard time not laughing himself. "I don't care how hot whatever you've got in there is—it's not going to keep us warm in *that*."

A silver moon, slightly more than half full, was shining down on an obsidian sea. It was the sea Adam was pointing to.

"It's not Ovaltine," Deborah told him impatiently. "It's something *we* mixed up."

The five boys were facing the girls, who were lined up behind Laurel. There was a bonfire going on the beach, but at this distance it did nothing to cut the icy wind.

"They're obviously not going to believe us," Faye said, and Diana added, "I guess we'll just have to show them."

Laurel passed the thermos around. Cassie took a deep breath and then a gulp. The liquid was hot and medicinal-tasting—like one of Laurel's nastier herbal teas—but the instant she swallowed it, a tingling warmth swept over her. Suddenly she didn't need her bulky sweater. It was positively hot out here on the beach.

"To the sea, ye mystics," Melanie said. Cassie wasn't sure what it meant, but like the other girls, she was shedding suddenly unnecessary clothing. The boys were goggling.

"*I* want a birthday party like this," Sean said urgently, as Faye unzipped her red jacket. "Okay? Okay? I want—"

The guys were mildly disappointed when it turned out the girls had bathing suits on underneath.

"But what are *we* supposed to do?" Adam said, sniffing at the thermos and grinning at the bikini-clad girls.

"Well . . ." Faye smiled. "You can always improvise."

"Or," Diana put in, "you can look behind the big rock. There just *might* be a pile of swimming trunks there."

"Now this really is different," Laurel said happily to Cassie some time later, while they were both floating in water up to their chins. "A midnight swimming party in November. This is *witchy*."

"Be more witchy if we were all sky-clad," Chris commented, shaking his shaggy blond head like a wet dog.

Cassie and Laurel looked at each other, then at Deborah, who was bobbing nearby.

"Good idea," Deborah said, nodding at the other girls. "How about you first, Chris?"

"Wait a minute—I didn't mean—hey,

Doug—*help!*"

"Come on, girls," Laurel shouted. "Chris wants to go skinny-dipping, only he's a little shy."

"Help! Guys, help!"

It turned into a sort of combination of tag and aquatic wrestling. Everyone joined in. Cassie found herself being chased by Nick and she fled, kicking up great splashes while he cut cleanly through the surf behind her. He got close enough to grab her.

"Help!" Cassie shrieked, half laughing, so that she accidentally drank some salt water. But there was no help in sight. Laurel and Deborah were heading an assault on the Henderson brothers, and Adam and Diana were far away, their sleek heads bobbing side by side.

Nick tossed wet hair—blacker than onyx in the moonlight—out of his eyes and grinned at her. Cassie had never seen him smile before. "Surrender," he suggested.

"Never," Cassie said, with as much dignity as she could muster while wavelets slapped her. Nick *was* handsome—but she didn't want him to get hold of her out here. He made another grab at her and Cassie shrieked for help again, and suddenly there was a heaving wave between them.

"Go on! Get out of here!" Faye said. Her eyes gleamed wickedly under long, wet lashes. "Or do we have to *make* you? Cassie, grab him around the neck while I get his trunks!"

Cassie had no idea how to grab a guy as strong as Nick around the neck, especially when she was laughing so hard, but she surged forward. Faye dove like a dolphin, and Nick twisted and made a hasty retreat, swimming away as fast as he could.

Cassie looked at Faye and found Faye smiling sideways at her. Cassie grinned.

"Thanks," she said.

"Any time," Faye said. "You know I'm glad to do anything for my friends. And we are friends, aren't we, Cassie?"

Cassie thought about that, treading water in the silver-glinting ocean. "I guess," she said, finally, slowly.

"That's good. Because, Cassie, there's a time coming up when I'm going to need all my friends. This Tuesday, when the moon is full, the Circle is going to have a meeting."

Cassie nodded, not getting it for a moment. Of course they were going to have a meeting. And another party; it was Faye's and Diana's birthday. They were both seventeen—

"The leadership vote!" Cassie said, taking an involuntary gulp of salt water again. She stared at Faye with a sudden terrible apprehension. "Faye . . ."

"That's right," Faye said. In the moonlight she looked like a mermaid, staying afloat effortlessly. Her glorious mane of hair hung soaking-wet down her back like twining seaweed. Her eyes held Cassie's. "I want to be leader of this coven, Cassie. I *will* be leader. And you're going to help me."

"No."

"Yes. Because this time I'm serious. I've been going easy on you, letting you have your way, not making you play by the rules. But that's over now, Cassie. This is the one thing I want more than anything else in the world, and you *are* going to help me. Otherwise . . ." Faye looked over her shoulder to where Adam and Diana were still bobbing, far away. Then she turned back.

"Otherwise, I'll do it," she said. "I'll tell Diana—and not just about that little cuddling session on the bluff. I'll tell her about the way you and Adam were kissing at the Homecoming dance—did you think nobody would see that?

And the *real* reason Adam went through four circles of protection to save you at Halloween. And"—she floated closer to Cassie, her hooded golden eyes as unblinking as the eyes of a falcon—"I'll tell her about the skull. How you stole it from her and gave it to me, so we could kill Jeffrey."

"That's not what happened! I'd never have let you have it if I'd known—"

"Are you sure, Cassie?" Faye smiled, a slow, conspiratorial smile. "I think, deep down, that you and I are just the same. We're . . . sisters under the skin. And if you don't vote for me on Tuesday, I'll let everyone know the truth about you. I'll tell them what you really are inside."

Evil, Cassie thought, staring out at the ocean. It reflected the moonlight back like a mirror, like a piece of hematite, and it surrounded her. She couldn't say a word.

"Think about it, Cassie," Faye said pleasantly. "You have until Tuesday night to decide." And then she swam away.

It was Tuesday night.

The full moon was directly overhead, the circle had been cast. The members of the Club sat around it. Diana, who was wearing all the symbols of the Queen of the Witches, had called on the four elements to protect them, but now she was silent. It was Melanie who was calling for the vote, from oldest to youngest.

"Nicholas," she said.

"I told you before," Nick said. "I won't vote. I'm *here*, because you two insisted"—he glanced from Faye to Diana—"but I abstain."

With a strange feeling of unreality, Cassie watched his handsome, cold face. Nick had abstained, why couldn't she? But she knew that would never satisfy Faye, unless Faye had already won. And Cassie was no closer to knowing which way to vote tonight than she had been three days ago. If only she had a little more time—

But there was no time. Melanie was speaking again.

"Adam."

Adam's voice was firm and clear. "Diana."

From a pile of red and white stones in front of her, Melanie put forward one white. "And as for me, I vote for Diana too," she said, and put out another white stone. "Faye?"

Faye smiled. "I vote for myself."

Melanie put out a red stone. "Diana."

"I vote for myself too," Diana said quietly.

A third white stone. Then Melanie said, "Douglas."

Doug grinned one of his wildest grins. "I'm voting for Faye, naturally."

"Christopher."

"Uh . . ." Chris looked confused. Despite Faye's frown and Doug's frantic coaching, he was squinting into nothingness as if searching for a lost decision. Finally, he seemed to find it and he looked at Melanie. "Okay; Diana."

Everyone in the circle stared at him. He glared back defiantly. Cassie's fingers clenched on the piece of hematite in her pocket.

"Chris, you feeb—" Doug began, but Melanie shut him up.

"No talking," she said, and put out a fourth white stone next to the two red. "Suzan."

"Faye."

Three red, four white. "Deborah."

"Who do you think?" Deborah snapped. "Faye."

Four red, four white. "Laurel," said Melanie.

"Diana's always been our leader, and she always will be," Laurel said. "I vote for her."

Melanie put a fifth white stone out, a trace of

a smile hovering on her lips. "Sean."

Sean's black eyes shifted nervously. "I . . ." Faye was staring at him relentlessly. "I . . . I . . . *Faye*," he said, and hunched up his shoulders.

Melanie shrugged and put out another red stone. Five red, five white. But although her gray eyes remained serious, her lips were definitely curved in a smile. All of Diana's adherents had relaxed, and they were flashing smiles at each other across the circle.

Melanie turned confidently to the last member of the coven and said, "Cassandra."

FOURTEEN

There was silence under the silver disk of moon.

"Cassie," Melanie said again.

Now everyone was looking at her. Cassie could feel the heat of Faye's golden eyes on her, and she knew why Sean had squirmed. They were hotter than the pillar of fire Diana had summoned up to protect them at Halloween.

As if compelled, Cassie glanced the other way. Diana was looking at her too. Diana's eyes were like a pool adrift with green leaves. Cassie couldn't seem to look away from them.

"Cassie?" Melanie said for the third time. Her voice was tinged with the slightest note of doubt.

Still unable to look away from Diana's eyes, Cassie whispered, "Faye."

"What?" cried Laurel.

"Faye," Cassie said, too loudly. She was clutching the piece of hematite in her pocket. Coldness from it seemed to seep through her body. "I said Faye, all right?" she said to Melanie, but she was still looking at Diana.

Those clear green eyes were bewildered. Then, all at once, understanding came into them, as if a stone had been tossed into the tranquil pool. And when Cassie saw that, saw Diana really *understand* what had just happened, something inside her died forever.

Cassie didn't know any longer why she was voting for Faye. She couldn't remember now how all this had started, how she'd gotten on this path in the first place. All she knew was that the coldness from her hand and arm was trickling through her entire body, and that from here on, there was no turning back.

Melanie was sitting motionless, stunned, not touching the pile of red and white stones. She seemed to have forgotten about them. It was Deborah who leaned forward and picked up the sixth red stone, adding it to Faye's pile.

And somehow that act, and the sight of the

six red stones beside the five white ones, made it real. Electricity crackled in the air as everyone sat forward.

Slowly, Melanie said, "Faye is the new leader of the coven."

Faye stood up.

She had never seemed so tall before, or so beautiful.

Silently, she held out a hand to Diana.

But it wasn't a gesture of friendship. Faye's open hand with the long crimson nails was *demanding*. And in response to it, very slowly, Diana got to her feet as well. She unclasped the silver bracelet from her upper arm.

Adam had been staring, thunderstruck. Now he jumped to his feet. "*Wait* a minute—"

"It's no use, Adam," Melanie said, in a deadened voice. "The vote was fair. Nothing can change it now."

Faye took the silver bracelet with the mysterious, runic inscriptions, and clasped it about her own bare, rounded arm. It shone there against the honey-pale skin.

Diana's fingers trembled as she undid the garter. Laurel, muttering something and brushing tears out of her eyes with an angry gesture, moved forward to help her, kneeling before Diana and tugging at the circle of green leather and blue silk. It came free and Laurel stood up, looking as if she wanted to throw it at Faye.

But Diana took it and placed it in Faye's hand.

Faye was wearing the shimmering black shift that she'd worn to the Halloween dance, the one slit up both sides to the hip. She buckled the garter around her left thigh.

Then Diana put both hands to her hair and lifted off the diadem. Fine strands of hair the color of sunlight and moonlight woven together clung to the silver crown as she removed it.

Faye reached out and almost snatched it from her.

Faye held the circlet up high, as if showing it to the coven, to the four elements, to the world. Then she settled it on her own head. The crescent moon in its center gleamed against her wild black mane of hair.

There was a collective release of breath from the Circle.

Cassie didn't know how she'd gotten to her feet, but suddenly she was running. She bolted out of the circle and ran beside the ocean, her feet sinking into wet sand. She ran until something caught her from behind and stopped her.

"Cassie!" Adam said. His eyes looked straight into hers, as if he was searching for her soul.

Cassie hit out at him.

"Cassie, I know you didn't want to do it! She made you, somehow, didn't she? Cassie, tell me!"

Cassie tried to shake him off again. Why was he bothering her? She was furious, suddenly, with Adam and Diana and their everlasting *faith* in her.

"I know she made you," Adam said forcefully.

"Nobody made me!" Cassie almost shouted. Then she stopped fighting him and they stood and stared at each other, both breathing hard.

"You'd better get back there," Cassie said. "We're not supposed to be alone—remember? Remember our oath? Not that I guess you *need* to think about it much anymore. It's pretty easy to keep these days, isn't it?"

"Cassie, what's going *on*?"

"Nothing is going on! Just go, Adam. Just—" Before Cassie could stop herself she had grabbed Adam's arms and pulled him forward.

And then she kissed him. It was a hard, angry kiss, and the next moment when she released him she was as stunned as he was.

They stared at each other speechlessly.

"Go back," Cassie said, hardly able to hear her own voice through the pounding in her ears. It was over, it was all over. She was so cold . . . not just her skin, but inside her, deep in her core, she was freezing. Freezing over like black ice. Everything was black around her.

She pushed Adam away and made for the distant glow of the bonfire.

"Cassie!"

"*I'm* going back. To congratulate our new leader."

It was chaos back at the circle. Laurel was crying, Deborah was shouting, Chris and Doug were glaring like a couple of tomcats about to fight and calling each other names. Sean was hovering behind Faye to keep his distance from a disdainful Melanie. Suzan was telling Chris and Doug to grow up, while Faye laughed. Of all of them, only Nick and Diana were utterly still. Nick was smoking silently, away from the rest of the group, watching them with narrowed eyes.

Diana was just standing there, exactly where

she'd been when Cassie left. She didn't seem to see or hear any of the disturbance around her.

"Will you all just shut up?" Deborah was yelling when Cassie reached them. "Faye's the one in charge now."

"That's right," Suzan said. Chris and Doug were shoving each other now. Suzan saw Cassie and said appealingly, "*Isn't* that right, Cassie?"

It was strange, how quickly the silence descended. Everyone was looking at Cassie again.

"That's right," Cassie said, in a voice hard as stone.

Chris and Doug stopped shoving. Laurel stopped crying. No one moved as Cassie walked over behind Faye. From that position she might have been supporting Faye—or she might have been about to stab her in the back.

If Faye was afraid, she didn't show it. "Okay," she said to the others. "You heard it. I'm leader. And now I'm going to give my first order." She turned her head slightly to address Cassie. "I want *you* to get the skull. As for the rest of you—we're going to the cemetery."

"*What?*" Laurel screamed.

"I'm leader and I'm going to *do* something with my power instead of just sitting on it. There's energy trapped in that skull, energy that we can use. Cassie, go get it."

Everyone was talking now, arguing, bellowing at each other. Things had never been like this when Diana was leader. Adam was yelling at Faye, demanding to know if she had gone crazy. Only Nick and Diana remained still, Nick watching, Diana staring at something only she could see.

Melanie was trying to restore calm, but it was doing no good. Some distant, clinical part of Cassie's mind noted that if Diana were to interfere now, if Diana would come forward and take over, the coven would listen to her. But Diana did nothing. And the shouting just got louder.

"*Get* it, Cassie," Faye was snarling between clenched teeth. "Or I'll get it myself."

Cassie could feel Power building around her. The sky overhead was stretched tight as a drum, tight as a harp string waiting to be plucked. The ocean behind her throbbed with pent-up force. She could feel it in the sand under her feet, and see it in the leaping flames of the bonfire.

She remembered what she'd done to the Doberman in the pumpkin patch. Some power had burst out from her, focused like a laser beam. Cassie felt as if something like that was concentrating in her now. She was connected to everything and it was all waiting for her to unleash it.

"Black John will let us have his power—he'll *give* it to us if we just ask the right way," Faye was shouting. "I *know*; I've communicated with him. But we have to go and ask him."

Communicated with him—when? Cassie thought. When she, Cassie, had let Faye take the skull the first time? Or at some point later?

"But why the *cemetery?*" Melanie was crying. "Why there?"

"Because that's what he *says*," Faye snapped back impatiently. "Cassie, for the last time! Get the skull!"

The elements were ranged behind her . . . Cassie stared at the back of Faye's neck. But then she remembered something. The look in Diana's eyes when Cassie had voted against her . . . oh, what good would it do to kill Faye now? Everything was over.

Cassie spun around and headed for the place where the skull was buried.

"How does she even know—?" Melanie was beginning, and Faye's laughter cut her off. So that was over, too, the secret about Cassie stealing the skull was out. Diana hadn't told anyone *exactly* where the skull was buried, not even Adam. Cassie ran so she wouldn't have to hear more.

She dug in the center of the blackened stones until her fingernails scraped the cloth that wrapped the skull. Then she dug around it and pulled it out of the sand, surprised, as always, by how heavy it was. Cassie staggered as she picked the skull up and started back to Faye.

Deborah ran to meet her. "This way," she said, diverting Cassie before she could reach the group. "Come on!" They climbed the bluff and Cassie saw Deborah's motorcycle.

"Faye planned this," Cassie said. She looked at Deborah, her voice rising slightly. "Faye had this planned!"

"Yeah. So what?" Deborah looked perplexed; a good lieutenant used to taking orders from her superior. What did Cassie care if Faye had it planned? "She figured she would have a hard time getting all the others to come, but she wanted to make sure we got there,"

Deborah explained.

"I don't see how she's going to get *any* of the others to come," Cassie said, looking down at the group below. But a strange madness seemed to have taken hold of some of them; whatever Faye was saying was whipping them into a frenzy. Suzan was heading for the bluff, and Doug was half dragging Chris. Faye was pushing Sean.

"That's seven; Faye said that's all we need," Deborah said, turning from the bluff. "Come on!"

This motorcycle ride was like the last, in that the speed was as great, the moon even brighter. But this time Cassie wasn't afraid, even though she could only hold on to Deborah with one arm. The other was hugging the skull to her lap. They reached the cemetery and a minute later heard engines. The Samurai was arriving with Chris and Doug and Suzan. Behind it was Faye's Corvette. Faye got out of the driver's side and Sean tumbled out of the passenger door.

"Follow me," Faye said. Long hair switching behind her, she made for the northeast corner. With every step she took, her bare, shapely legs flashed pale, showing the garter on her thigh and a black-handled dagger tucked in the garter. When the ground began to rise, she stopped.

Cassie stopped, too, clutching the skull to her chest with both arms, frighteningly aware of where they were standing. In a row here, broken only by a mound in the earth, were the graves of Faye's father, Sean's mother, and all the other dead parents from Crowhaven Road. Sean was sniveling now, and only Deborah's grip on him was keeping him from running away.

Faye turned to face them. Even in the worst of times, the tall, dramatically beautiful girl had a natural authority, an ability to intimidate people. Now that seemed enhanced by the symbols of the Queen of the Witches: the diadem, the bracelet, the garter. An aura of power and glamour surrounded her.

"It's time," Faye said, "to take back the energy that belonged to the original coven, and that Black John stored in the skull. Black John wants us to have that power, to use against our enemies. And we can get it back—*now*."

Taking the black-handled dagger out of her garter, Faye unsheathed it and drew a quick, imperfect circle in the dried-up grass. "Get in," she said, and the others took their places.

She's got them moving so fast they're not thinking about what they're doing, Cassie thought. No one questioned Faye; everyone seemed caught up in the driving urgency Faye was creating. Even Sean had stopped whining and was staring, rapt.

And Faye made a stunning sight as she held the knife up and rapidly called on the elements for protection. Too fast, Cassie was thinking— such slight protection when all their efforts on Halloween hadn't been enough. But she couldn't speak either; they were all caught on a roller-coaster ride and nobody could stop it. Least of all Cassie, who was so numb and cold . . .

"Put the skull in the center, Cassie," Faye said. Her voice was breathless and her chest was rising and falling quickly. She looked more excited than she had ever looked about Jeffrey, or Nick, or that guy from the pizza place she'd taken upstairs.

Cassie knelt and placed the cloth-wrapped thing in the middle of Faye's flawed circle.

"And now," Faye said, in that queer, exultant voice, staring down at the sandy lump between her feet, "we can reclaim the power that should have been ours all along. I call on all the elements to witness—"

"Faye, stop!" Adam shouted, appearing running between the gravestones.

The rest of the coven was behind him, including Diana, who still looked as if she were moving in her sleep. Even Nick, silent and watchful as always, was in the rear.

Faye snatched up the covered skull and held it cradled in her two hands. "You had your chance," she said. "Now it's my turn."

"Faye, just stop a minute and *think*," Adam said. "Black John isn't your friend. If he's really communicated with you, whatever he's told you is lies—"

"*You're* the liar!" Faye shot back.

"Chris, Doug—that skull killed Kori. If you let that dark energy loose again—"

"Don't listen to him!" Faye shouted. She looked like some barbarian queen as she stood there, long legs apart, silver glinting against the black of her shift and the darker black of her hair. Cassie realized that while Adam was talking to her, Laurel and Melanie were circling, one on either side.

Faye realized it, too. "I won't let you stop me! This is the beginning of a new Circle!"

"*Please*, Faye—" Diana cried, desperately,

seeming to wake up at last.

"By Earth, by Air, by Fire, by Water!" Faye shouted, and she jerked the cloth off the skull and held it in both hands over her head.

Silver. The full moon shone down on the crystal and seemed to blaze there, and it was as if another face were suspended above Faye's; a livid, unnatural, skeletal face. And then— darkness began to pour forth from it. Something blacker than the sky between the stars was streaming out of the skull's eyesockets, out of its gaping nose-hole and between its grinning teeth. Snakes, thought Cassie, staring hypnotized at what was happening. Snakes and worms and the old kind of dragons, the kind whose heavy scales scrape the ground and who spit poison when they breathe. Everything bad, everything black, everything loathsome and crawling and evil seemed to be flooding out of that skull, although none of it was real. It was only darkness, only black light.

There was a sound like the humming of bees, only higher, more deadly. It was growing. Faye was standing under that dreadful cascade of darkness, and the sound was like two ice picks driving into Cassie's ears, and somewhere a dog was barking . . .

Someone has to stop this, Cassie realized. No—*I* have to stop this. *Now*.

She was getting to her feet when the skull exploded.

Everything was quiet and dark.

Cassie wanted it to stay that way.

Somebody groaned beside her.

Cassie sat up slowly, looking around, trying to piece together what had happened. The cemetery looked like a killing field. Bodies were strewn all over. There was Adam, stretched out with one arm reaching toward the circle and Raj beside him. There was Diana with her shining hair in the leaves and dirt. There was Nick, getting to his hands and knees, shaking his head.

Faye was lying in a pool of black silk, her dark hair covering her face. Her hands with their long red nails were cupped, open—but empty. There was no sign of the skull.

Someone groaned again, and Cassie looked to see Deborah sitting up, rubbing her face with one hand.

"Are they dead?" Deborah said hoarsely, staring around.

"I don't know," Cassie whispered. Her own

throat hurt. All those bodies, and the only movement was the fluttering of Diana's hair in the wind. And Nick, who was stumbling toward the circle.

But then there was a stirring—people were starting to sit up. Sean was whimpering. Suzan was, too. Deborah crawled over to Faye and pushed Faye's hair back.

"She's breathing."

Cassie nodded; she didn't know what to say. Adam was bending over Diana—she looked quickly away from that. Melanie and Laurel were up, and so were Chris and Doug, looking like punch-drunk fighters. Everyone seemed to be alive.

Then Cassie saw Laurel gasp and point. "Oh, my *God*. The mound. Look at the mound."

Cassie turned—and froze. Her eyes went back and forth over the scene without believing it.

The mound her grandmother had told her was for storing artillery was broken open. The rusty padlock was gone, and the iron door was jammed against the piece of concrete. But that wasn't all. The top of the mound, where the sparse cemetery grass had grown, was cracked like an overripe plum. Like the cocoon of an insect that had burst free.

And all up and down the line of graves by the fence, tombstones were tilting crazily. The ones nearest the mound, the ones with the names of the parents of Crowhaven Road, were split and shattered. *Riven*, Cassie thought, the old-fashioned word coming from nowhere, singularly appropriate.

Something from inside the mound smelled bad.

"I've got to see," Deborah muttered. Cassie had never admired anyone so much as she did Deborah just then, making her staggering way toward the open mound. Deborah had more physical courage than anyone Cassie had ever known. Dizzily, Cassie got up and lurched beside her, and they both fell to their knees at the edge of the evil-smelling fissure.

The moon shining inside showed that it was empty. But there was a coating like slime on the raw earth down there.

Then light and motion caught Cassie's eye.

It was in the sky, the sky to the northeast. It was something like the aurora borealis, except that it flickered intermittently, and it was entirely red.

"That's above Crowhaven Road," Nick said.

"Oh, God, what's happening?" Laurel cried.

"Looks like fire," Deborah muttered, still hoarse.

"Whatever it is, we'd better get there," Nick said.

Adam was holding Diana, trying to revive her. Suzan and Sean were huddled, and Chris and Doug still looked punchy. But Melanie and Laurel were on their feet, if shaken.

"Nick's right," Melanie said. "Let Adam take care of things here. Something's happening."

Cassie glanced at Faye, her fallen leader, lying on the ground. Then she turned and followed Melanie without a word.

It didn't matter that the five who started unsteadily toward the road had just recently been on opposite sides of a fight. There was no time to think about anything that petty now. Cassie got on the back of Deborah's motorcycle, and Melanie and Laurel jumped into Nick's car. The others would have to follow when they could—and if they wanted to.

Wind roared in Cassie's ears like the sound of the sea. But the feeling of power she'd had earlier, the connection with the elements, was broken. She couldn't *think*—her mind was fuzzy and cloudy as if she had a bad cold. All she knew was that she had to get to Crowhaven Road.

"It's not fire," Deborah shouted as they approached. "No smoke."

Dark houses flew by—Diana's, Deborah's. The empty Georgian at Number Three. Melanie's, Laurel's, Faye's. The vacant Victorian. The Hendersons', Adam's, Suzan's, Sean's . . .

"It's at your house, Cassie," Deborah shouted.

Yes. Cassie knew it would be. Something inside her had known even before they started out.

A maple tree showed up like a black skeleton against the red light that engulfed the house at Number Twelve. But the red wasn't fire. It was some witch-light, a crimson aura of evil.

Cassie remembered how much she had hated this house when she'd first seen it. She'd hated it for being huge and ugly, with its peeling gray clapboards and its sagging eaves and unwashed windows. But now she cared about it. It was her family's ancient home; it belonged to her. And more important than anything, her mother and grandmother were inside.

FIFTEEN

Cassie jumped off the motorcycle and ran up the driveway. But as soon as she entered the red light, she slowed. Something about the light made it hard to move through it, hard even to breathe. It was as if the air here had thickened.

In slow motion, Cassie fought her way to the door. It was open. Inside, the ordinary lights, the lamps in the hallway, looked feeble and silly against the red glow that pervaded everything, like flashlights in the daytime.

Then Cassie saw something that made her breath catch.

Footprints.

Something had tracked mud across her

grandmother's pine-board floor. Only it wasn't mud. It was black as tar and it steamed slightly, like some primordial muck from hell. The prints went up the stairs and then back down again.

Cassie was afraid to go any farther.

"What is this?" Nick shouted, coming in behind her. His shout didn't go very far in the thickened air; it sounded muffled and dragging. Cassie turned toward him, and it was like turning in a dream, where every motion is reduced to a crawl.

"Come on," Nick said, pulling at her. Cassie looked behind her and saw Deborah and Melanie and Laurel in the doorway, also moving in slow motion.

Cassie let Nick guide her and they fought their way up the stairs. The red glow was dimmer up here; it was hard to see any prints. But Cassie followed them more by intuition than by sight down the hall to the door of her mother's room, and she pointed to it. She was too frightened to go in.

Nick's hand grasped the doorknob, turned it. The door slowly flew open. Cassie stared at her mother's empty bed.

"*No!*" she screamed, and the red light seemed

to catch the word and draw it out endlessly. She forgot to be frightened then and ran forward—slowly—into the middle of the room. The bed was rumpled, slept-in, but the covers had been thrown back and there was no sign of her mother.

Cassie looked around the deserted room in anguish. The window was closed. She had a terrible sense of loss, a terrible premonition. Those black and steaming footprints went to the side of her mother's bed. Some *thing* had come and stood here, beside her mother, and then . . .

"Come on! Downstairs," Nick was shouting from the doorway. Cassie turned to him—and screamed.

The door was swinging slowly shut again. And in the shadows behind it was a pale and ghostly figure.

Cassie's second scream was cut off as the figure stepped forward, showing a drawn white face and dark hair falling loose over slender shoulders. It was wearing a long, white nightgown. It was her mother.

"*Mom,*" Cassie cried, and she launched herself forward, throwing her arms around her mother's waist. Oh, thank God, thank God, she thought. Now everything would be all right. Her mother was safe, her mother would take care of things. "Oh, Mom, I was so scared," she gasped.

But something was wrong. Her mother wasn't hugging her back. There was no response at all from the upright but lifeless body in the nightgown. Cassie's mother just *stood* there, and when Cassie pulled back, she saw her mother was staring emptily.

"Mom? *Mom?*" she said. She shook the slender white figure. "*Mom!* What's the matter?"

Her mother's beautiful eyes were blank, like a doll's eyes. Unseeing. The black circles underneath seemed to swallow them up. Her mother's arms stayed limp at her sides.

"Mom," Cassie said again, almost crying now.

Nick had pushed the door open again. "We have to get her out of here," he told Cassie.

Yes, Cassie thought. She tried to convince herself that it was the light, that maybe outside of the red glow her mother would be okay. They each took one of the limp arms and led the unresisting figure into the hallway. Melanie, Laurel, and Deborah converged from different directions.

"We looked in all the rooms on this floor," Melanie said. "There's no one else up here."

"My grandmother—" Cassie began.

"Help us get Mrs. Blake downstairs," Nick said.

At the bottom of the stairs, the black prints turned left and then crossed and recrossed. A thought flashed into Cassie's mind.

"Melanie, Laurel, can you take my mom outside? Out of the light? Will you make sure she's safe?" Melanie nodded, and Cassie said, "I'll be out as soon as I can."

"Be *careful*," Laurel said urgently.

Cassie saw them leading her mother to the door, then she made herself stop looking. "Come on," she said to Nick and Deborah. "I think my grandma's in the kitchen."

A line of footprints led that way, but it wasn't just that, it was a *feeling* Cassie had. A terrible feeling that her grandmother was in the kitchen, and that she wasn't alone.

Deborah walked like a stalking huntress, following the black marks down the twisting hallways to the old wing of the house, the one built by the original witches in 1693.

Nick was behind Cassie, and Cassie realized vaguely that they were protecting her, giving her the safest place in line. But there was no safe place in this house now. As they crossed the threshold into the old wing, the red light seemed to get stronger, and the air even thicker. Cassie felt her lungs laboring.

Oh, God, it *looked* like fire in here. The red light was everywhere and the air burned Cassie's skin. Deborah stopped and Cassie almost ran into her. She struggled to see over Deborah's shoulder, but her eyes were sore and streaming.

She felt Nick behind her, his hand gripping her shoulder hard. Cassie tried to make her eyes focus, squinting into the thick red light.

She could see her grandmother! The old woman was lying in front of the hearth, by the long wooden table she had worked at so often. The table was on its side, and herbs and drying racks were scattered on the floor. Cassie started toward her grandmother, but there was something else there, something her mind didn't want to take in. Nick was holding her back, and Cassie stared at the thing bending over the old woman.

It was burned, black, hideous. It looked as if its skin was hard and cracked. It had the shape of a man, but Cassie couldn't see eyes or clothes or hair. When it looked up at them she got a brief, terrifying impression of a skull shining silver through the blackness of its face.

It had seen them now. Cassie felt as if she and Nick and Deborah were welded together; Nick was still holding her, and she was clutching Deborah. She wanted to run, but she *couldn't*, because there was her grandmother on the floor. She couldn't leave her grandmother alone with the burned thing.

But she couldn't fight, either. She didn't know how to fight something like this. And Cassie could no longer feel any connection to the elements; in this horrible oven of a room she felt as if she were cut off from everything outside.

What weapons did they have? The hematite in Cassie's pocket wasn't cool anymore; when she thrust her hand in to touch it, it burned. No good. Air and Fire and Earth were all against them. They needed something this creature didn't control.

"Think of water," she shouted to Nick and Deborah. Her voice was stifled in the oppressive blistering air. "Think of the ocean— cold water—ice!"

As she said it, she thought herself, trying to

remember what water was like. Cool . . . blue. . . endless. Suddenly she remembered looking over the bluff when she'd first come to her grandmother's house, seeing a blue so intense it took her breath away. The ocean, unimaginably vast, spread out before her. She could picture it now; blue and gray like Adam's eyes. Sunlight glinted off the waves, and Adam's eyes were sparkling, laughing . . . .

Wind rattled the windows in their casements, and the faucet in the sink began to shake. It burst a leak somewhere at its base and a thin stream of white water sprayed up. Something burst in the dishwasher, too, and water gushed on the floor. Water was hissing out of the pipe under the sink.

"Now!" Deborah shouted. "Come on, get him now!"

Cassie knew it was wrong even as Deborah said it. They weren't strong enough, not nearly strong enough to take this thing on directly. But Deborah, always heedless of danger, was lunging forward, and there was no time to scream a warning or make her stop. Cassie's heart failed her and her legs went weak in the middle of the rush toward the black thing.

It would kill them—one touch of those

burned, hardened hands could kill—but it was giving way before them. Cassie couldn't believe they were still alive, still moving, but they were. The thing was backing away, it was crouching, it was running. It turned and went through what had been the old front door, searing the handle black as it went. It went out into the darkness and then it was gone.

The door hung open, rattling in the wind. The red light died. Through the doorway Cassie could see the cool silver-blue of moonlight.

She dragged in a deep breath, grateful just to be able to breathe without hurting.

"We did it!" Deborah was laughing. She pounded Nick on the arm and back. "We did it! All right! The bastard ran!"

It *left*, Cassie thought. It left, deliberately. We didn't win anything.

Then she turned sharply to Nick. "My mother! And Laurel and Melanie—they're out there—"

"I'll go check them. I think it's gone for now, though," he said.

For now. Nick knew the same thing she did. It wasn't defeated; it had withdrawn.

On trembling legs, Cassie went and knelt by

her grandmother on the floor.

"Grandma?" she said. She was afraid the old woman was dead. But no, her grandmother was breathing heavily. Then Cassie was afraid that if the wrinkled eyelids opened, the eyes underneath would stare blankly like a doll's— but they were opening now, and they saw her, they knew her. Her grandmother's eyes were dark with pain, but they were rational.

"Cassie," she whispered. "Little Cassie."

"Grandma, you're going to be all right. Don't move." Cassie tried to think of anything else she'd heard about injured people. What to do? Keep them warm? Keep their feet elevated? "Just hang on," she told her grandmother, and to Deborah she said, "Call an ambulance, fast!"

"*No,*" her grandmother said. She tried to sit up and her face contracted with pain. One knobby-knuckled hand clutched at the thin robe over her nightgown. Over her heart.

"Grandma, don't move," Cassie said frantically. "It's going to be all right, everything's going to be all right . . ."

"No, Cassie," her grandmother said. She was still breathing in that tortured way, but her voice was surprisingly strong. "No ambulance.

There's no time. You need to listen to me; I have something to tell you."

"You can tell me later." Cassie was crying now, but she tried to keep her voice steady.

"There won't *be* a later," her grandmother gasped, and then she settled back, her breathing careful and slow. She spoke distinctly, kneading Cassie's hand in her own. Her eyes were so dark, so anguished—and so kind. "Cassie, I don't have much time left, and you need to listen. This is important. Go to the fireplace and look on the right-hand side for a loose brick. It's just about the level of the mantel. Pull it out and bring me what's inside the hole."

Cassie stumbled to the hearth. A loose brick—she couldn't *see*; she was crying too hard. She felt with her fingers, scraping them on the roughness of mortar, and something shifted under them.

This brick. She dug her fingernails into the crumbled mortar around it and worked it back and forth until it came out. She dropped it and reached into the cool dark hollow now exposed.

Her fingertips found something smooth. She eased it closer with her nails, then grasped it and pulled it out.

It was a Book of Shadows.

The one from her dream, the one with the red leather cover. Cassie took it back to her grandmother and knelt again.

"He couldn't make me tell where it was. He couldn't make me tell anything," her grandmother said, and smiled. "My own grandmother showed me that was a good place to hide it." She stroked the book, then her age-spotted hand tightened on Cassie's. "It's yours, Cassie. From my grandmother to me to you. You have the sight and the power, as I did, as your mother does. But you can't run away like she did. You have to stay here and face him."

She stopped and coughed. Cassie looked at Deborah, who was listening intently, and then back at her grandmother. "Grandma, *please*. Please let us call the ambulance. You can't just give up—"

"I'm not giving anything up! I'm giving it all to *you*. To you, Cassie, so you can carry on the fight. Let me do that before I die. Otherwise it's all been meaningless, everything." She coughed again. "It wasn't supposed to be like this. That girl—Faye—she fooled me. I didn't think she would move this fast. I thought we would have more time—but we don't. So, now listen."

She drew a painful breath, fingers holding Cassie's so hard it hurt, and her dark old eyes stared into Cassie's. "You come from a long line of witches, Cassie. You know that. But you don't know that our family has always had the clearest sight and the most power. We've been the strongest line and we can see the future— but the others don't always believe that. Not even our own kind."

Her eyes lifted to look at Deborah. "You young people, you think you come up with everything new, don't you?" Her seamed old face wrinkled in a laugh, although there was no sound. "You don't have much respect for old folks, or even for your parents. You think we lived our lives standing still, don't you?"

She's wandering, Cassie thought. She doesn't know what she's saying. But her grandmother was going on.

"Your idea about getting out the old books and reviving the old traditions—you think you were the only ones to come up with that, don't you?"

Cassie just shook her head helplessly, but Deborah, brows drawn together in a scowl, said,

"Well, weren't we?"

"No. Oh, my dears, no. In my day, when I was a little girl, we played with it. We had meetings sometimes, and those of us with the sight would make notes of what we saw, and those with the healing touch would talk about herbs and things. But it was your parents' generation who got up a real coven."

"Our *parents?*" Deborah said in disbelief. "My parents are so scared of magic they practically puke if you mention it. My parents would *never*—"

"That's now," Cassie's grandmother said calmly, as Cassie tried to hush Deborah. "That's now. They've forgotten—they made themselves forget. They had to, you see, to survive. But things were different when they were young. They were just a little older than you, the children of Crowhaven Road. Your mother was maybe nineteen, Deborah, and Cassie's mother was just seventeen. That was when the Man in Black came to New Salem."

"Grandma . . ." Cassie whispered. Icy prickles were going up and down her spine. This room, which had been so hot, was making her shiver. "Oh, Grandma, please . . ."

"You don't want to know. I know. I

understand. But you have to listen, both of you. You have to understand what you're up against."

With another cough, Cassie's grandmother shifted position slightly, her eyes going opaque with memory. "That was the fall of 1974. The coldest November we'd had in decades. I'll never forget him on the doorstep, kicking the snow off his boots. He was going to move into Number Thirteen, he said, and he needed a match to light the wood he was carrying. There was no other kind of heat in that old house; it had been empty since he'd left it the first time."

"Since *what?*" Cassie said.

"Since 1696. Since he'd left the first time to go to sea, and drowned when his ship went down." Her grandmother nodded without looking at Cassie. "Oh, yes, it was Black John. But we didn't know that then. How much suffering could have been prevented if we *had* . . . but there's no use thinking about that." She patted Cassie's hand. "We lent him matches, and the girls and young men on the street helped him rebuild that old house. He was a few years older than they were, and they looked up to him. They admired him and his travels— he could tell the most marvelous stories. And he was handsome—handsome in a way that didn't show his black heart underneath. We were all fooled, all under his spell, even me.

"I don't know when he started talking to the young people about the old ways. Pretty soon, I guess; he worked fast. And they were ready to listen. They thought we parents were old and stodgy if we opposed them. And to tell the truth, not many of us objected very strongly. There's good in the old ways, and we didn't know what *he* was up to."

The shivers were racing all over Cassie's body by now, but she couldn't move. She could only listen to her grandmother's voice, the only sound except for the thin hiss of water in that quiet kitchen.

"He got the likeliest of the young ones together and paired them off. Yes, that's about the size of it, although we parents didn't know then. He made matches, giving this girl to this boy, and this boy to that girl, and somehow he made it all seem reasonable to them. He even broke up pairs that had planned to marry—your mother, Deborah, was going to marry Nick's dad, but *he* changed that. Switched her from one brother to the other, and they let him. He had such a grip on them they would have let him do anything.

"They did the marriages in the old way, handfasting. Ten weddings in March. And we all celebrated, like the idiots we were. All those young people so happy, and never a quarrel between them, we thought; how lucky they were! They were just like one big group of brothers and sisters. Well, the group was *too* big for one coven, but we didn't think about that.

"It was good to see the respect they had for the old ways, too. They had the Beltane fire in May and at midsummer they gathered Saint-John's-wort and mistletoe. And in September I remember all of them laughing and shouting as they brought the John Barleycorn sheaf in to represent the harvest. They didn't know what the other John was planning.

"We knew by then the babies were coming soon, and that was another reason to celebrate. But it was in October that some of the older women started to worry. The girls were all so pale and the pregnancies seemed to take so much out of them. Poor Carmen Henderson was flesh and bones except for her belly. *That* looked like she was carrying twin elephants. There wasn't much celebrating at Samhain; the girls were all too sick.

"And then on November third, it started. Your uncle Nicholas, Deborah, the one you never knew, called me to come to his wife's bedside. I helped Sharon have little Nick, your cousin. He was a fighter from the first minute; I'll never forget how he squalled. But there was something else, something I'd never seen in a baby's eyes, and I went home thinking about it. There was a *power* there I'd never seen before.

"And two days later it happened again. Elizabeth Conant had a baby boy, with hair like Bacchus's wine and eyes like the sea. That baby *looked* at me, and I could feel his power."

"Adam," Cassie whispered.

"That's right. Three days later Sophie Burke went into labor—her that kept her own name even when she married. Her baby, Melanie, was like the others. She looked two weeks old when she was brand-new, and she saw me as clearly as I saw her.

"The strangest ones born were Diana and Faye. Their mothers were sisters and they had their babies at the same moment, in two separate houses. One baby was bright like sunlight and the other one was dark as midnight, but those two were connected somehow. You could tell even at that age."

Cassie thought of Diana and a pang went through her, but she pushed it away and went on listening. Her grandmother's voice seemed to be getting weaker.

"Poor little things . . . it wasn't their fault. It isn't *your* fault," the old woman said, focusing suddenly on Deborah and Cassie. "Nobody can blame you. But by December third, *eleven* babies had been born, and they were all strange. Their mothers didn't want to admit it, but by January there was no way to deny it. Those tiny babies could call on the Powers, and they could scare you if they didn't get what they wanted."

"I knew," Cassie whispered. "I knew it was too weird for all of those kids to born within one month . . . I *knew*."

"Their parents knew, too, but they didn't know what it meant. It was Adam's father, I think, who put it all together for them. Eleven babies, he said—he guessed that with one more that made a coven. And who was the one more? Why, the man who'd arranged for all those babies to be born, the man who was going to lead them. Black John had come back to make the strongest Circle this country had ever seen—not from this generation, but from the next, Adam's father said. From the infants.

"Nobody believed the story at first. Some parents were scared, and some were just plain stupid. And some didn't see how Black John could come back from the dead after all those years. That's one mystery that hasn't been solved yet.

"But gradually some of the group were convinced. Nick's father, who'd lost his own fiancée, seen her married off to his younger brother—he listened. And Mary Meade, Diana's mother; she was as smart as she was pretty. Even Faye's father, Grant Chamberlain . . . he was a cold man, but he knew his infant daughter could set the curtains on fire without touching them, and he knew that wasn't right. They got some of the others talked around, and one cold night, the first of February, the bunch of them set off to talk to *him* about it."

SIXTEEN

Cassie's grandmother shook her head. "To talk! If they'd come to us, to the older women, we might have warned them. Me and Laurel's grandma, and Adam's grandma, and Melanie's great-aunt Constance—we could have told them a few things, maybe saved them. But they went alone, without telling anyone. On Imbolc, February first, more than half the group that *he* had put together went to challenge him. And out of that group, not one came back."

Tears were running slowly down the seamed old cheeks. "So you see, it was the brave ones, the strong ones that went and died. The ones that are left are the ones too scared or too stupid to see the danger—I'm sorry, Deborah, but it's true." Cassie remembered that both Deborah's parents were alive. "All the best of Crowhaven Road went to fight Black John that Imbolc Night," her grandmother said.

"But how?" Cassie whispered. She was thinking of that row of gravestones in the cemetery. "How did they die, Grandma?"

"I don't know. I doubt if anyone alive knows, unless it's . . ." Her grandmother broke off and shook her head, muttering. "There was fire in the sky, and then a storm. A hurricane from the sea. The older women got together the babies that had been left with them, and the young parents that hadn't gone with the group, and we managed to save them. But the next day the house at Number Thirteen was burned to the ground, and all the ones who'd gone to challenge Black John were dead.

"We never found most of the bodies. They were washed out to sea, I suppose. But one thing we did find was the burned corpse at Number Thirteen. We knew it was *him* by the ring he wore, a shiny black stone we used to call lodestone. I forget the modern name. We took *him* out to the old burying ground and put him in the bunker. Charles Meade, Diana's father, dropped that chunk of concrete in front of it. We figured that if he'd come back once, he might try again someday, and we meant to stop him if we could. And after that the parents that had survived hid their Books of Shadows and did their best to keep their children away from magic. And it's strange, but most of them forgot what they could. I guess because they couldn't remember and stay sane. Still, it's funny, now, how much they've forgotten."

The cracked voice had been growing weaker and weaker, but now Cassie's grandmother grasped Cassie's wrist hard. "Now, listen to me, child. This is important. Some of us didn't forget, because we couldn't. I'd named my daughter for a prophetess, and she did the same for her daughter, because we've always had the second sight. Your mother couldn't bear what her gift showed her, and so she ran away from New Salem; she ran all the way to the other coast. But I stayed, and I've watched all my premonitions come true, one by one. The babies that were born on Crowhaven Road in that single month grew up different, despite everything their parents could do. They were drawn to the Powers and the old ways from the beginning. They all grew up strong—and some of them grew up bad.

"I've watched it happen, and in my mind I've heard Black John laughing. They burned his body, but they couldn't burn his spirit, and it's always been here, waiting, hanging around the old burying ground and the vacant lot at Number Thirteen. He was waiting for his coven, the one he'd planned, the one he'd gotten born. He was waiting for them to come of age. He was waiting for them to bring him back.

"I knew it would happen—and I knew only one thing could stand against him when it did. And that's *you*, Cassie. You have the strength of our family, and the sight, and the Power. I begged your mother to come home, because I knew that without you the children of Crowhaven Road would be lost. They'd turn to *him*, the way their parents did, and he'd be their leader and their master. You are the only one who can stop him from taking them now."

"So that's what you and Mom fought about," Cassie said in wonder. "About *me*."

"We fought about courage. She wanted to protect you, and I knew that by protecting you we'd lose all the others. You had a destiny even before you were born. And the worst was that we couldn't tell you about it—that was what the prophecies said. You had to come here all unknowing and find your own way, like some innocent sacrifice. And you did. You've done everything we could have wanted. And the time was coming when we could have explained it all to you . . . but she fooled us, that Faye. By the way, how'd she do it?"

"I . . ." Cassie didn't know what to say. "I helped her, Grandma," she said finally. "We found the crystal skull that belonged to Black John, and it was full of dark energy. Every time we used it, somebody died. And then—" Cassie took a deep, ragged breath. "Then, tonight, Faye told us to bring the skull to the cemetery. And when she uncovered it there—I don't know—all this darkness came out . . ."

Cassie's grandmother was nodding. "*He* was master of dark things. Just like the real Man in Black, the lord of death. But, Cassie, do you really understand?" With a supreme

288

effort, the old woman tried to sit up to look in Cassie's face. "When you took the skull to his burying place and let that energy out, it was enough to bring him back. He's *here* now; he's come back again. Not a ghost or a spirit, but a man. A walking, breathing man. He'll look different the next time you see him; once he's had a chance to pretty himself up. And he'll try to fool you." She sank back wearily.

"But, oh, Grandma—I helped let him loose. I'm sorry. I'm so sorry . . ." Tears swam in Cassie's eyes.

"You didn't know. *I* forgive you, child, and what's done is done. But you have to be ready for him . . ." Cassie's grandmother's eyes drifted shut, and her breath had a frightening sound.

"Grandma!" Cassie said, shaking her in panic.

The old eyes opened again, slowly. "Poor Cassie. It's a lot to face. But you have strength, if you look for it. And now you have this." Feebly, she pressed the Book of Shadows again into Cassie's hands. "The wisdom of our family, and the prophecies. Read it. Learn it. It'll answer some of the questions I don't have time for. You'll find your way . . ."

"Grandma! Grandma, *please* . . ."

Her grandmother's eyes were still open, but they were changing, filming over, as if they didn't see her anymore. "I don't mind going now that I've told the story . . . but there's something else. Something you need to know . . ."

"Cassie!" The voice came from the doorway, and it startled Cassie so much that she jerked and looked up. Laurel was standing there, her elfin face white with concern. "Cassie, what's *happening* in here? Are you okay? Do you want a doctor?" She was staring at Cassie's grandmother on the floor.

"Laurel, not now!" Cassie gasped. She was crying, but she held on harder to her grandmother's knotted old hands. "Grandma, please don't go. I'm frightened, Grandmother. I *need* you!"

Her grandmother's lips were moving, but only the faintest of sounds came out. ". . . never be afraid, Cassie. There's nothing frightening in the dark if you just face it . . ."

"Please, Grandma, please. Oh, *no* . . ." Cassie's head dropped down to her grandmother's chest and she sobbed. The knotted hands weren't holding hers anymore.

"You said you had something else to tell me," she wept. "You can't go . . ."

An almost inaudible breath came from her grandmother's chest. Cassie thought it was the word "John." And then, ". . . nothing dies forever, Cassie . . ."

The chest against Cassie's forehead heaved once and was still.

Outside, a yellowing moon hung low in the sky.

"The Mourning Moon," Laurel said quietly. "That's what this one is called."

It was appropriate, Cassie thought, although her eyes were dry now. There were more tears inside her, building up, but they would have to wait. There was something that had to be done before she could rest and cry. Even after her grandmother's story, she had so many questions, so much to figure out—but first, she had to do this one thing.

There were a bunch of cars parked near the street. The rest of the coven was there—no, not all of them. Cassie saw Suzan and Sean and the Hendersons, and Adam and Diana. But she didn't see the person she was looking for.

"Melanie and Nick took your mom to Melanie's aunt Constance," Laurel said hesitantly. "They thought it was the best place for her, tonight. She was still kind of spacey—but I know she'll be okay."

Cassie swallowed and nodded. She *wasn't* sure; she wasn't sure of anything. She only knew what she had to do right now.

Never be afraid, Cassie. There's nothing frightening in the dark if you just face it.

Just face it. Face it and stand up to it.

Then Cassie saw who she was looking for.

Faye was in the shadows beyond the headlights of the cars. Her black shift and her hair blended in with the gloom, but the pallor of her face and the silver ornaments she wore stood out.

Cassie walked up to her without hesitation. At that moment, she could have hit Faye, strangled her, killed her. But all she said was, "It's over."

"What?" Faye's eyes gleamed a little, yellow as the moonlight. She looked sick and unsettled—and dangerous. Like a pile of dynamite ready to go off.

"It's over, Faye," Cassie repeated. "The blackmail, the threats . . . it's all over. I'm not your prisoner anymore."

Faye's nostrils flared. "I'm warning you, Cassie, this isn't the time to push me. I'm still leader of the coven. The vote was fair. You can't do anything to change it . . ."

"I'm not trying to change it—*now*. Right now I'm just saying that you don't have a hold over me anymore. It's finished."

"It's finished when *I* say it's finished!" Faye snarled. Cassie realized then how close Faye was to snapping, how dangerous Faye's mood really was. But it didn't matter. Maybe it was even better this way, to get it all over with at once.

"I'm not joking, Cassie," Faye was going on heatedly. "If you can turn on me, I can do the same to you . . ."

Cassie took a deep breath and then said, "Go ahead."

There's nothing frightening in the dark if you just face it.

"Fine," Faye said between her teeth. "I will."

She turned around and strode to the place where Diana and Adam were standing, arms around each other. Adam was practically supporting Diana, Cassie saw, and for a moment her heart failed her. But it had to be done. Despite the oath, despite Diana's pain, it had to be done.

Faye turned back once to look at Cassie. A look that said, clearly, *you'll be sorry*. Cassie wondered in sudden panic if it was true. Would she be sorry? Was she doing the wrong thing after all, defying Faye at the wrong time? Wouldn't it be better to wait, to think about this . . .

But Faye was turning back to Diana, malicious triumph written all over her face. The coven wasn't happy with Faye tonight, but Faye was still the leader and nothing could change that fact. Now Faye was going to start her reign by getting revenge on the people she hated most.

"Diana," she said, "I have a little surprise for you."

Don't miss the shocking conclusion of
THE SECRET CIRCLE
Volume III
The Power

"Diana, I have a little surprise for you," Faye said.

Diana's emerald eyes, with their thick, sooty lashes, were swimming already. She still hadn't recovered from the shocks of tonight, and her face was strained as she stared at Faye.

Well, there was worse to come.

Now that it was finally going to happen, Cassie felt a curious sense of freedom. No more trying to hide, no more lying and evading. The nightmare was here at last.

"I suppose I should have told you before, but I didn't want to upset you," Faye was saying. Her eyes burned golden with a savage inner fire.

Adam, who wasn't stupid, glanced from Cassie to Faye and obviously came to a quick, if shattering conclusion. He swiftly cupped a hand under Diana's elbow.

"Whatever it is can wait," he said. "Cassie ought to go and see her mother, and—"

"No, it can't wait, Adam Conant," Faye interrupted. "It's time Diana found out what sort of people she has around her." She whirled to face Diana again, her pale skin glowing with strange elation against the midnight-dark mane of her hair. "The ones you've chosen," she said to her cousin. "Your dearest friend—and him. The incorruptible Sir Adam. Do you want to know the reason you couldn't make it as leader? Do you want to know how naive you really are?"

Everyone was gathering close now, staring. Cassie could see varying degrees of bewilderment and suspicion in their expressions. The full moon shining from the west was so bright that it cast shadows, and it illuminated every detail of the scene.

Cassie looked at each of them: tough Deborah, beautiful Suzan with her perfect face marred by a puzzled frown, cool Melanie, and graceful, elfin Laurel. She looked at Chris and Doug Henderson, the wild twins, who were standing by the slinking figure of Sean, and at icily handsome Nick behind them.

Finally she looked at Adam.

He was still holding Diana's arm, but his proud, arresting face was tense and alert. His eyes met Cassie's, and something like understanding flashed between them, and then Cassie looked away, ashamed. She had no right to lean on Adam's strength. She was about to be exposed for what she was in front of the entire Circle.

"I kept hoping they would do the decent thing and control themselves," Faye said. "For their own sake, if not yours. But, obviously—"

"Faye, what are you talking about?" Diana interrrupted, her patience splintering.

"Why, about Cassie and Adam, of course," Faye said, slowly opening her golden eyes wide. "About how they've been fooling around behind your back."

The words fell like stones into a tranquil pool. There was a long moment of utter silence, then Doug Henderson threw back his head and laughed.

"Yeah, an' my mom's a topless dancer," he jeered.

"And Mother Theresa's really Cat-woman," said Chris.

"Come on, Faye," Laurel said sharply. "Don't be ridiculous."

Faye smiled.

"I don't blame you for not believing me," she said. "I was shocked too. But you see, it all started before Cassie came to New Salem. It started when she met Adam down on Cape Cod."

The silence this time had a different quality. Cassie saw Laurel look quickly at Melanie. Everyone knew that Cassie had spent several weeks that summer on the Cape. And everyone knew that Adam had been down in that area too, looking for the Master Tools. Cassie saw the dawning of startled understanding on the faces around her.

"It all started on the beach there," Faye went on. She was obviously enjoying herself, as she always enjoyed being the center of attention. She looked sexy and commanding as she wet her lips and spoke throatily, addressing the entire group although her words were meant for Diana. "It was love at first sight, I guess—or at least they couldn't keep their hands off each other. When Cassie came up here she even wrote a poem about it. Now how did that go?" Faye put her head on one side and recited:

"Each night I lie and dream about the one
Who kissed me and awakened my desire
I spent a single hour with him alone
And since that hour, my days are laced with fire."

"That's right; that was her poem," Suzan said. "I remember. We had her in the old science building and she didn't want us to read it."

Deborah was nodding, her petite face twisted in a scowl. "I remember too."

"You may also remember how strange they both acted at Cassie's initiation," Faye said.

"And how Raj seemed to take to Cassie so quickly, always jumping up on her and licking her and all. Well, it's very simple really—it's because they'd known each other before. They didn't want any of us to know that, of course. They tried to hide it. But eventually they got caught. It was the night we first used the crystal skull in Diana's garage—Adam was taking Cassie home, I guess. I wonder how that got arranged."

Now it was the turn of Laurel and Melanie to look startled. Clearly they remembered the night of the first skull ceremony, when Diana had asked Adam to walk Cassie home, and Adam, after a brief hesitation, had agreed.

"They thought they were alone on the bluff—but somebody was watching. Two little somebodies, two little friends of mine . . ." Lazily, Faye worked her fingers, with their long, scarlet-tipped nails, as if stroking something. A flash of comprehension lighted Cassie's mind.

The kittens. The damned little bloodsucking kittens that lived wild in Faye's bedroom. Faye was saying the kittens were her spies? That she could communicate with them?

Cassie felt a deeper chill as she looked at the tall, darkly beautiful girl, sensing something alien and deadly behind those hooded golden eyes. She'd wondered all along who Faye had meant when she talked about her "friends" that saw things and reported back to her, but she'd never imagined this. Faye smiled in satisfaction and nodded at her.

"I have lots of secrets," she said directly to Cassie. "That's only one of them. But anyway," she said to the rest of the group, "it was that night they got caught. They were—well, kissing. That's the polite way to put it. The kind of kissing that starts spontaneous combustion. I suppose they just couldn't resist their lustful passions any longer." She sighed.

Diana was looking at Adam now, looking for a denial. But Adam, his jaw set, was staring straight ahead at Faye.

Diana's lips parted with the quick intake of her breath.

301

"And it wasn't the only time, I'm afraid," Faye continued, examining her nails with an expression of demure regret. "They've been doing it ever since, stealing secret moments when you weren't looking, Diana. Like at the Homecoming dance—what a pity you weren't there. They started kissing right in the middle of the dance floor. I guess maybe they went somewhere more private afterward . . ."

"That's not true," Cassie cried, realizing even as she said it that she was virtually confirming that everything else Faye had said *was* true.

Everyone was looking at Cassie now, and there was no more jeering from the Hendersons. Their tilted blue-green eyes were focused and intent.

"I wanted to tell you," Faye said to Diana, "but Cassie just begged me not to. She was hysterical, crying and pleading—she said she would just die if you found out. She said she'd do anything. And that," Faye sighed, looking off into the distance, "was when she offered to get me the skull."

"What?" said Nick, his normally

imperturbable face reflecting disbelief.

"Yes." Faye's eyes dropped to her nails again, but she couldn't keep a smile from curling the corners of her lips. "She knew I wanted to examine the skull, and she said she'd get it for me if I didn't tell. Well, what could I do? She was like a crazy person. I just didn't have the heart to refuse her."

Cassie sank her teeth into her lower lip. She wanted to scream, to protest that it hadn't been that way . . . but what was the use? Faye's story had enough of the truth in it to condemn her.

Melanie was speaking. "And I supose you didn't have the heart to refuse the skull either," she said to Faye, her gray eyes scornful.

"Well . . ." Faye smiled deprecatingly. "Let's put it this way—it was just too good a chance to miss."

"This isn't funny," Laurel cried. She looked stricken. "I still don't believe it—"

"Then how do you think she knew where to dig up the skull tonight?" Faye said smoothly. "She stayed over at your house,

Diana, the night we traced the dark energy to the cemetery. And she snuck around and figured out where the skull was buried by reading your Book of Shadows—but only after she stole the key to the walnut cabinet and checked there." Gleeful triumph shone out of Faye's golden eyes; she couldn't conceal it any longer.

And nobody in the group could deny the truth of Faye's words any longer. Cassie *had* known where to dig up the skull. There was no way to get around that. Cassie could see it happening in face after face; the ending of disbelief and the slow beginning of grim accusation.

It's like *The Scarlet Letter*, Cassie thought wildly as she stood apart with all of them looking at her. She might as well be standing up on a platform with an "A" pinned to her chest. Helplessly, she straightened her back and tried to hold her chin level, forcing herself to look back at the group. I will not cry, she thought. I will not look away.

Then she saw Diana's face.

Diana's expression was beyond stricken.

She seemed simply paralyzed, her green eyes wide and blank and shattered.

"She swore to be loyal and faithful to the Circle, and never to harm anyone inside it," Faye was saying huskily. "But she lied. I suppose it's not surprising, considering she's half outsider. Still, I think it's gone on long enough; she and Adam have had enough time to enjoy themselves. So now you know the truth. And now," Faye finished, looking over the ravaged members of the Circle, and especially her deathly still cousin, with an air of thoughtful gratification, "we'd probably better be getting home. It's been a long night." Lazily, smiling faintly, she started to move away.

"No." It was a single word, but it stopped Faye in her tracks and it made everyone else turn toward Adam.

Cassie had never seen his blue-gray eyes look this way before—they were like silver lightning. He moved forward with his usual easy stride and there was no violence in the way he caught Faye's arm. But the grip must have been like iron—Cassie could tell that because Faye couldn't get away from it. Faye looked down at his fingers in offended surprise.

"You've had your turn," Adam said to her. His voice was carefully quiet, but the words dropped from his lips like chips of white-hot steel. "Now it's mine. And all of you" —he swung around on the group, holding them in place with his gaze— "are going to listen."

☷ **HarperPaperbacks** *By Mail*

A brother and sister must come to terms with their family's
unthinkable legacy.

And don't miss these other terrifying thrillers:

Love You to Death by Bebe Faas Rice
Julie is looking for a change in her dull high school routine. When sexy and
mysterious Quinn comes to town, it looks like her problems are solved. But
Quinn is the jealous type. And when Julie's friends start disappearing, she fears
that her new love may be more of a change than she bargained for.

The Dark by M. C. Sumner
Shiloh Church doesn't believe the scary legends about Rue Cave—but when the
members of her archaeological dig start dying, Shiloh discovers that the cave
holds a terrifying, deadly secret.

The Cheerleaders by John Hall *
Holly Marshall is looking forward to her senior year, especially trying out for
Harding High's cheerleading squad. But when she starts getting phone calls
from a dead classmate, everyone thinks she's crazy—maybe even crazy enough to
commit murder!

* coming soon